Praise for *The Arm*

"Ruthless and heart-wrenching."   —Robin Hobb

"Cole weaves . . . a fantasy world that feels comfortably familiar, then goes to places you'd never expect. You won't stop turning pages until the stunning finish."   —Peter V. Brett

"Brutal and lovely—an inventive and poignant fantasy that's rich with keen characters, set in a vivid, fascinating world."
                                                   —Cherie Priest

"A dark fantasy tale with sharp teeth and a hard punch. Heloise is the hero we need, and Myke Cole is the writer to bring her transformation to light."   —Chuck Wendig

"Intelligently written, fun, and brutal in equal measures."
                                                   —Mark Lawrence

"A most satisfying fantasy, with terrific action sequences."
                                        —B&N Sci-Fi & Fantasy Blog

"Dark but well depicted."   —RT Book Reviews

"Cole has created a dark medieval world that by the end only has a small sliver of light in it. . . . A must-read for fans of Erika Johansen's Queen of the Tearling series."
                                        —Booklist (starred review)

ALSO BY MYKE COLE

THE SACRED THRONE TRILOGY
The Queen of Crows

SHADOW OPS TRILOGY
Control Point
Fortress Frontier
Breach Zone

THE REAWAKENING TRILOGY
Gemini Cell
Javelin Rain
Siege Line

THE ARMORED SAINT

MYKE COLE

A TOM DOHERTY ASSOCIATES BOOK

NEW YORK

THE ARMORED SAINT

Copyright © 2018 by Myke Cole

Edited by Justin Landon

A Tor.com Book
Published by Tom Doherty Associates
175 Fifth Avenue
New York, NY 10010

www.tor.com

Tor® is a registered trademark of Macmillan Publishing Group, LLC.

The Library of Congress Cataloging-in-Publication Data
is available upon request.

ISBN 978-1-250-19967-6 (trade paperback)
ISBN 978-0-7653-9594-8 (ebook)

Our books may be purchased in bulk for promotional, educational, or business use. Please contact your local bookseller or the Macmillan Corporate and Premium Sales Department at 1-800-221-7945, extension 5442, or by email at MacmillanSpecialMarkets@macmillan.com.

First Edition: February 2018
First Trade Paperback Edition: September 2018

Printed in the United States of America

0 9 8 7 6 5 4 3 2 1

For Nzinga of Ndongo, Gudit, and Running Eagle.
For the Trung Sisters and Teuta.
For Emilia Plater, Razia Sultana, and Vishpala.
For Jeanne d'Arc and Boudicca and on and on and on.

Women, red in tooth and claw.

The strong have done what they could. Now the weak will suffer what they must.

—*Thucydides*

I

THEY'LL HEAR YOU

*And it shall be as a plague unto your people
From father to son, from mother to daughter, until your
   seed is dust.
My redemption is the Emperor. My hope is His
   outstretched hand.
He has made my way plain, and asked only this of me,
Suffer no wizard to live.*
            —Writ. Ala. I. 14

Heloise took her father's hand, squeezing it hard. Samson's eyebrows lifted as he squeezed hers back. "Been a long time since you took your old father's hand. What happened to you being nearly a woman grown?"

The warm roughness of his palm made her feel safe, but she only smiled up at him, shrugged.

"The road to Hammersdown's the safest in the valley," her father said. "No bandit'd risk running into the Order."

"It's the Order that scares me."

"Me, too," Samson agreed, "but they're a sight better than a wolf pack or a robber band, eh?"

She didn't want to hear that something frightened him now. She wanted Samson the father and protector, not Samson the friend. Her father was a big man, and if his hair had gone gray and his stomach drooped over his belt, he more than made up for it with his broad shoulders and thick hands. For all his talk of being frightened, Samson's eyes were hard, "Serjeant's eyes," the village Maior called them. He had fought alongside her father in the Old War. *Don't let his factor's hands fool you, Heloise. Your father was a shield-hewer, the strongest pikeman I've ever known. The very name Samson struck terror into the hearts of the Emperor's enemies.*

"Well." Samson pulled her into an embrace, holding her tightly to his side as they walked, his arm strong and comforting. "This old man will take what he can get."

"I love you, Papa . . ."

"I love you, too, dove."

Hoofbeats.

Samson stopped, glanced over his shoulder. Heloise turned.

Dust was rising on the road, billowing out behind a column of riders. Too many to be bandits, even if they were brave enough to risk the Order's main road. Heloise heard jangling chains and looked for a cart, but couldn't see one.

"Papa, what's . . ."

The dust whirled and cleared to reveal Pilgrims, their gray cloaks flapping away from leather armor, flails held out before them. At their head rode a Sojourner. His cloak was edged with gold, the bright red fabric so clean it shone, as if the dust dared not touch him.

The Sojourner held his flail across his chest, head over one shoulder, black iron spikes nestled against the scarlet fabric of his cloak. The red meant he had completed the great Sojourn, a year on the road to visit the sites where the Emperor had fought the devils until they were pushed back into hell. The Pilgrims' gray marked them as lesser men who'd done only the fortnight-long

Pilgrimage. They were pale imitations of their leader, their cloaks simple.

Only their flails were equal: the same stout, well-oiled wood. The same sturdy, black length of chain.

The Order had arrived, as if talk of them had made them appear.

She heard her father gasp in recognition, and then he was yanking her out of the road and into the chill mud. Heloise fell to her knees, winced from the cold wet seeping into her dress. "Eyes down," Samson said, "mouth closed."

The terror was as intense as it was sudden.

She obeyed him, closing her mouth and casting her eyes to the ground. The cool air felt suddenly hot, the wide sky pressing down on them.

The hoofbeats came closer, and with them, the sound of the jangling chains.

"Bow your head, girl, now!" Samson hissed.

The hoofbeats seemed to continue endlessly. The sound of the chains rose as they drew closer. Heloise could see the links playing out behind the horses, dragging in the dirt. A dead woman slid past Heloise, green and bloated, caked with road filth. She was wrapped in the long, gray ropes of her innards, tangled in the metal links until Heloise couldn't tell her guts from the chains. The horses dragged another body beside her, wrapped in metal like a silkworm in molt.

Heloise's gorge rose at the stink and she gagged, clapping a hand to her mouth. Another moment and they would be past. *Please don't notice us. Please ride on.*

The jangling ceased as the riders halted.

Heloise couldn't resist glancing up. The Sojourner had a narrow face and a smile that was somehow worse than a scowl. He slowly turned his horse, a black animal taller and broader than any Heloise had ever seen. Heloise felt fear climb her spine, followed by anger at him for making her afraid.

"You, there," the Sojourner called to Samson. "Attend me."

Samson rose, eyes still on the ground. "Your eminence."

"You live here?"

"Yes, your eminence. We hail from Lutet, just up the—"

"I know where Lutet is," the Sojourner said. "What I need to know is where Frogfork is."

"If you ride on past the Giant's Shoulder," Samson said, "you will see a carter's track through the woods. Take it until the ground goes to marsh, then head into the mire. You'll see it."

"Can we make it by nightfall?"

"Yes, my lord. If you ride without stopping."

"Very well. In that case, have you anything in that satchel to slake my thirst? Maybe some bread? I will pray a cycle for your soul and the Emperor will bless you for supporting His own Hand in the valley."

"I'm sorry, your eminence. I am a factor on my way to take letters."

"That is not an answer to my question."

"All I have is my ledger, pen, and ink."

"He's a villager, Holy Father," one of the Pilgrims said. "They are bred to lie."

He turned to Samson, held out a hand. "Give it here."

Without lifting his eyes, Samson handed the satchel over.

The Pilgrim fumbled with the iron buckle before cursing and ripping it open, sending a popped rivet flying. He thrust one gauntleted hand inside and seized a handful of her father's pens, tossed them into the mud. One of the inkpots followed.

Heloise's mind whirled, calculating the cost of the precious items, figuring how they could be repaired. It wasn't so bad. The pens were wood and metal. Some had fine tips, but provided she was careful when she cleaned them, they wouldn't be damaged. She winced as the inkpot struck the wet mud, but she didn't think it had cracked. So long as he didn't throw out any of the . . .

The Pilgrim's hand disappeared back into the satchel, emerged with a handful of crumpled paper. Heloise was only able to half-stifle a cry as he tossed the precious sheets in the air. They drifted in the wind, made their way down toward the wet mud.

Before Heloise knew what she was doing, she had taken a long, lunging step, her hand lashing out to grasp at the falling paper. The sudden move stirred the wind, and the precious sheets danced away from her, floating sideways and down, always down, until the ground snatched them up. Heloise chased them, knowing it was useless, unable to stop herself, eyes locked on the slowly spreading stain that was wet mud hungrily devouring the tools of her trade.

A hoof stomped in the mud so close that she had to leap back, her eyes darting up to catch the Pilgrim's. They were a dazzling gray-blue, like the skim of ice over flowing water. "What in the Emperor's name do you think you are doing?"

Heloise straightened, panic blossoming in her gut. "Just picking up the . . . I only meant to pick up the paper before it got wet."

"Heloise!" Samson said.

"Your eminence," she added.

"If the paper is on the ground," the Pilgrim said, "it's because I meant it to be there."

Even now, Heloise had to fight not to bend down and pick the paper up. *He only threw out some of it*, she told herself. *It's not all ruined.* The thought helped her to be still.

The Sojourner leaned on his saddle horn, gestured to the bodies in the chains behind them. "See that, girl?"

Heloise glanced back at the bodies. She knew she should

answer, but she was robbed of speech, first by fear, then by rage. The Sojourner's smile slowly faded as he waited.

Samson's elbow in her ribs. "Answer him!"

"Yes."

Her father's elbow in her ribs once more, almost knocking her over. "Your eminence," Heloise added again.

The Sojourner nodded, whether for the elbowing or at her answer, she couldn't tell. "Such is the fate of wizards and those who give shelter to wizards. They betrayed the Emperor."

The Sojourner gestured to the corpses with one red-gloved hand. "This is why the Writ counsels obedience above all, girl. For a chance at power, they would have rent the veil and let the devils walk among us. Is this not more than they deserve?"

Heloise looked sideways at her father, but his eyes were on the ground, his jaw clenched.

Heloise looked back to the corpse. The dead woman's tongue had swollen out of her mouth, fat and gray. The moment dragged on. The Sojourner had asked her a question, she had to answer.

She pictured herself wrapped in those chains, dragged behind a horse. Her lips moved by themselves. "No, your eminence."

The Sojourner straightened, satisfied. His small smile returned. "Very well. Brother Tone, I take it there is nothing of use in that rag?"

The Pilgrim looked up from Samson's satchel. "No, Holy Father. The villager speaks truth, for once."

"Let's get moving then. He is likely speaking truth about the ride to Frogfork as well."

"Yes, Holy Father." Brother Tone turned his horse, throwing the satchel over his shoulder as he went.

Heloise watched it turn end over end, the lid flapping open, the remaining papers threatening to fall out. She could see the wind plucking at them, ready to cast them down to join their comrades in the ruinous mud. She felt herself start to cry then, because it was the rest of what they had, because she knew that most of their earnings for the next season would have to go to replenish their supply, because . . .

She heard a dull thud, felt something soft strike her hands.

Her father's eyes widened and the remains of the Sojourner's smile vanished.

Heloise looked down at the satchel nestled in her outstretched arms. She had moved. She had caught it. "I'm sorry . . ." Her lips felt numb. She didn't know why she'd done it. It was as if her body had been unable to accept the outcome, not when it could do something about it. "I didn't mean . . ."

"Perhaps you do not understand what the Holy Writ means by 'obedience.'" The Sojourner's voice was cold. His spurs jingled as he touched them to his horse and the animal took a step toward her.

"Please, your eminence." Samson moved between them. "She's only a girl."

Brother Tone twitched the reins and pulled his horse between Samson and the Sojourner.

"She's near a woman grown," the Pilgrim said, his blue eyes blazing. "Old enough to know what she's doing."

"Please, your eminence," Samson said, looking up now. "She's my only child."

Tone sat up straight, hands tightening on his flail. "Come here. Show me your eye."

"Holy Brother, there's no—" Samson began.

"Your. Eye." The Pilgrim cut him off. "Open it."

Heloise reached for her father, but he placed a broad hand on her belly, shoving her back. With the other, he reached up to his right eye, prying it wide open with thumb and forefinger.

Tone looked for a long time. At last he sat back, turned to his master, nodded.

"I see no portal," the Sojourner agreed. "There is no wizardry here, only pride and the foolish love of a father for his child. Your first love should be the Emperor. Above all things."

"Yes, Holy Brother." The relief in Samson's voice made Heloise angry and sad at the same time.

"You're lucky we've pressing business," the Pilgrim said, tugging his horse back into the column. "Otherwise, I'd teach you a lesson."

"Yes, Holy Brother," Samson said again, but it was lost in the pounding of hoofbeats, the jangling of chains, and the rising dust as the riders started moving again. Heloise and Samson stood, silent and frozen, as the whole column trundled into the distance, until at last they turned with the road and moved out of sight.

Samson didn't take his hand from Heloise until the hoofbeats had faded. Heloise glared after them.

"Bastards," Samson said, patted the dust from his trousers. Then he turned to Heloise, his face lit with fury. "Idiot girl! What in the Emperor's name were you thinking?"

Heloise had thought she couldn't be more frightened, but her father's hot anger was somehow worse than the Sojourner's cool threats. "I'm sorry, Papa!" She held out the satchel, showing the dry sheets safe inside. "I saved some . . ."

Samson's eyes flicked from her to the satchel and back again. He took a long, shuddering breath and the anger in his eyes vanished as he exhaled. "So you did, girl. So you did."

He looked at her face and sighed, put his hands on her shoulders. "Heloise, I know you were trying to help, but that was very, very foolish. That could have turned out badly for both of us."

"I'm sorry, Papa," she said again, "I don't know why I did it, I just . . . but paper is so costly and I thought that . . . he was finished with it . . ." The fear and the humiliation swirled in her mind and her gut, so intense that she almost missed a third, stronger emotion, boiling beneath it all.

Rage. Fury at the Order for making her father grovel while they destroyed the tools of his trade.

"No buts," he cut her off. "That was reckless. When a killer dumps your kit in the mud, you smile sweetly and tell him he's done right."

The anger wouldn't let her. "But he hasn't done right, Papa. And the Writ says—"

"That a word of truth is more pleasing to the Emperor than poetry, yes. I know the Writ as well as you. But it doesn't change that however pleasing it may be to the Emperor's ears, it isn't to the Sojourner's, and he's the one with the flail."

Heloise's stomach churned. She had seen dead animals before, and been graveside for funerals more than once. But the image of the dead woman's face still hung in her mind. Her father was right, she had put him in danger. "I'm sorry, Papa."

Samson embraced her. "From now on, when the Order's about, you're a statue, mind me? Still as a stone. Answer their questions and that's all. Now, help me clean up this mess."

They cleaned the mud off the pens as best they could. The inkpot was whole, if a bit dirty. The paper was so thoroughly soaked that it was hard to distinguish from the mud, and they left it where it lay, walking on in silence.

Her father was right. She had risked both of their lives. As Heloise considered it, the anger turned from the Order to herself.

Samson looked at her, smiled grimly. "What's done is done, Heloise. Don't drive yourself mad about it."

"Yes, Papa," Heloise said, but she could hear the shame in her voice.

Samson put a gentle hand on her shoulder. "What does the Writ tell us about the light of the Sacred Throne?"

"That we bask in its radiance always," Heloise answered from memory, "that the Emperor's light warms and blinds in equal measure."

"That's so." Samson nodded. He jerked his thumb up at the sun. "And there it is, shining over us all. No matter what happened, try and take joy in the day, girl. We have precious few of them."

Heloise did her best, trying to feel the warmth of the sun on her face the rest of the way to Hammersdown, but the sour feeling stayed in her stomach, and her father's kindness made her feel even worse. She almost wished he'd shout at her, tell her she was a fool who could have gotten them both killed.

She opened her mouth to apologize again when she heard shouts. Growing louder.

"It sounds like Churic," Heloise said.

Her father nodded. "Something's got him stirred."

Churic's voice grew louder as they walked past Hammersdown's sentry tower. Heloise heard other voices now, Jaran Trapper, and Bertal Fletcher, too.

Alna Shepherd stood at the common's far end. His dog, Callie, had rounded the sheep into a tight circle. She stood in front of them, a low growl in her throat, until Alna's daughter Austre patted the dog into silence.

Jaran stood beside Bertal. The two were practically identical, lined faces nearly hidden behind thick gray beards. Jaran was distinguished only by his gold chain of office, marking him as Maior. Both men were bent over Churic, red-faced and shouting.

Churic was simple, dressed in rags. He'd lived on Hammersdown's charity his entire life, rocking back and forth on the village green. Heloise's mother said that Churic's mother had lustful thoughts so the Emperor had taken Churic's mind when he was still in the womb. As long as Heloise had known Churic, he'd been as gentle as the sheep Callie protected, but now his face was purple, his words running together until they formed a single long shout, "Nuhnuhnuhnuhnuhnuh."

"Shut your damn hole!" Jaran shouted back. "Sacred Throne, what's gotten into you?"

Bertal looked up, saw Samson, and traded a long look with Jaran before putting on a forced smile. "Samson Factor! As I live and breathe. Good to see you!"

Samson let go of Heloise's hand. She fought the urge to reach for his again.

"We had some trouble on the road," Samson said. "All's well here?"

Bertal smiled so broadly, it looked like his cheeks hurt. He glanced nervously at Churic. "Of course all's well! Why don't we head to my shop and get to business, eh? Marda's made some meat pies." Samson's eyes stayed on Churic. There was spit on the simpleton's lips now, white and foaming.

Austre jogged over to them. She was two winters older than Heloise, long black curls framing her face. She had taken a woman's shape more quickly than Heloise, taller and fuller. Her eyes were dark and beautiful, but they were too wide, her face pale. "Hello, Master Factor. Would Heloise like to come play with Callie until you're done? Papa's about to take the flock in and I've the afternoon to gather hoxholly. I've got my betrothal dress too!" She said to Heloise, "Would you like to see it?"

Samson glanced distractedly at Austre. "Thank you, Austre, but Heloise is here today as my apprentice. She's to be working as well."

"Oh," Austre said. "Well, maybe she can come later?" Heloise was happy to see her, and felt a stab of disappointment at missing the chance to run Callie through the tall grasses on the common, but the pall of fear that hung over the village made it short-lived.

"Look!" Churic jumped to his feet, prying his eye wide. "See the portal? I'm a gateway! Hell comes through me! The devils will soon be here!"

Samson froze. "What did he say?"

"Churic!" Jaran shouted, grabbing Churic's shoulders. "Shut your damn yob and shut it now!"

But Churic wouldn't stop. "Wizard! Look! I'm a wizard! I bring hell to you all!"

"What in the shadow of the Throne is this?" Samson's eyes went hard.

"It's nothing!" Bertal said. "Mad ravings, is all. You know old Churic." The fletcher laughed. Heloise thought it sounded more like a scream.

"Hell!" Churic chanted. "Wizard! Devil! The portal in my eye! The portal in my eye!"

"Damn you!" Jaran yelled, hurling Churic to the ground and kneeling on his chest, hands locked around his throat. "You will shut up or by the Emperor I will strangle you and leave you for the wolves."

"Don't hurt him!" Heloise started forward, but Samson grabbed her collar, pulling her back.

Churic kicked, gurgling.

"Your girl's got a kind heart. Nothing wrong with that!" Bertal said. "Anyway, that's all sorted. Let's to business."

"I'll not do business today," Samson grunted.

"Papa," Heloise began, thinking of the paper they'd lost to the mud.

"Samson," Jaran called to him, loosening his grip so Churic could take a whooping breath. "It's nothing."

Samson stabbed an angry finger in the Maior's direction. "That is *not* nothing. That is burning talk. I'll not have dealings anywhere near it."

"It's sorted!" Jaran shouted. "We both need the custom. Don't leave without trade."

"He said 'wizardry,'" Samson said. "He said he had the portal in his eye."

"He's a madman!" Jaran let Churic draw another breath, tightened his grip again before he could speak.

"Come on." Austre tugged on Heloise's hand. "Let's leave the men to handle this and . . ."

"It was the *Order* that troubled us on the road!" Samson shouted, pushing Heloise behind him. "They're about, might even be close enough to hear! Ask them if they care for the mad!"

"You don't have to choke him!" Heloise said, struggling, her father's big hand holding her fast.

"Damn you, Samson!" the Maior shouted. "We both know he's no wizard! He's mad!"

"And we both know that doesn't matter," Samson replied. "The Order won't care. They'll Knit you. And you're not even a day's walk from my home and hearth, you bastard. I'll not have my family Knit because you can't keep a muzzle on your dog."

Jaran's face turned white, red spots showing on his cheeks. "Samson . . ."

"No more talk. You'd best choke him until he stops kicking," Heloise's father seethed, "or cut out his tongue and run him out. For our sake if not your own."

"He's simple," Jaran said. "He'll die out there."

"Then that is as the Emperor wills," Samson snarled. "Better him than mine."

Samson turned and dragged Heloise so hard that she had to

take great, leaping steps to keep up with him. Callie set to barking, a steady, accusing stream that followed them out to the trail home.

Heloise was quiet for a long time, anger at the injustice warring with her fear of the look on her father's face.

They walked without speaking for as long as Heloise could stand. "Papa, the Maior said he wasn't a wizard. There was no portal in his eye. The Order would have seen that, even if they came."

Samson only shook his head, the fury in his eyes fading to sadness.

The look made her bold. "That's the truth, isn't it? Churic isn't a wizard, he's just simple?"

"Yes." Samson nodded. "Jaran spoke truth."

"Then why . . ." Heloise began.

"Better to Knit than permit," Samson recited from the Writ. "What happens if Churic really is a wizard and the Order lets it pass?"

"The portal in his eye opens and the devils come through," Heloise recited from memory. "But he's not a wizard."

"Aye"—her father nodded—"but it doesn't matter. Churic's life, the lives of all of Hammersdown are nothing against what would be lost should a devil come through the veil. If there's even the smallest chance that Churic might be telling truth, the Order cannot risk it. Remember this. If you ever hear words of wizardry, loose talk of the veil or what lies beyond, you run straight to me, you hear? Better that we handle it in the village than let it pass to the Order. Remember what you saw on the road today. That is what comes of letting matters like this go unattended."

She remembered the words of the Writ. *This we believe: That the Emperor stood for all mankind during the great battle for the future of the world. That He cast the devils back into hell. That, gravely wounded, He used the last of His life to draw the veil shut between the world and hell, sealing the devils away forever. He died and was reborn as the divine Imperial Soul, immortal, His unblinking eye ever turned on the safety of His empire, on keeping the veil shut.*

For a thousand years, humanity had known not peace, but life at least, which was more than they could expect should the devils return.

But sometimes, they did return.

There were men and women who thought themselves above the Imperial Writ, who wanted the wizardry that flowed like water in hell, who were willing to reach beyond the veil to get it. Such people knew great power for a time, but sooner or later, the portal in their eye would open, and they would turn from people into doorways, and the devils would come through.

Suffer no wizard to live.

When a wizard was discovered, the Order came to put the matter right. They took no chances. Even talk of wizarding meant there was a chance the veil had been rent.

And what was rent, must be Knit.

"Will they kill him, Papa?" Heloise asked. "Will they cut out his tongue?"

Samson looked sad. "They will if they are wise, but men are soft when it comes to their own. Churic may be simple, but he is someone's son, and Jaran would not have kept him through so many winters if there wasn't at least one in Hammersdown with sympathy for the man."

"Are the devils so bad? Have you ever seen one?" Heloise asked.

"No one has, poppet. No one but the Order."

"Then how do we know they're real?" Heloise asked.

Samson looked annoyed. "Because the Writ tells us, girl. Because the Order reminds us. The devils are real, and they are terrible, and we must be ever vigilant for their return."

That didn't make sense, but what Heloise wanted was to feel safe, to feel like she and her father were on the same side, and so all she said was, "Yes, Papa."

There was a part of Heloise's stomach that churned and whirled, a sick ball deep in her middle. That part could not forget the dead woman's face, her swollen tongue gray, and cracked lips. That part told Heloise that even though her father's words made a cruel kind of sense, this wasn't the way things were supposed to be.

2

TINKER'S FORGE AND RANGER'S GIFT

Our Captain-General is a Lyse Alderman. Goes by Shrop-shire, I think. These city lords aren't named for their trade. His badge is a winged Palantine, a sainted devil-slayer. This is meant to comfort the levy, I think, but it's off. Palantines are devil-slayers, aye. But not one of them survived the contest.

—from the journal of Samson Factor

The journey home took the rest of the day. Hammersdown had chilled them both, and Samson spoke no more of taking joy in the day, or of anything else, not even humming to fill the silence as he always did. Heloise clung to his hand, needing the safety that his calloused palm conveyed, even if it did make her feel like a child.

When at last the Lutet sentry tower reared above the treetops, Samson cupped his hands and shouted. "'Ware the tower! Wake up, Danad, you old idiot."

But it was the face of Danad's son, Ingomer, that appeared over the wooden edge. "Sorry, Master Factor. I must have dozed off."

"Your secret's safe with me, young master Clothier. Where's the Maior?"

"With the Tinkers, I think," Ingomer said. "What news from the road?"

"The Order is riding for Frogfork, and Churic's finally flipped his cap. Could mean trouble."

"Let me know what the Maior says."

Samson grunted assent and led Heloise beneath the tower's broad beams. Their house was in the shadow of the tower, but Samson turned away from it and up the rutted track that led from the common green to the Tinkers' workshop. "When did Ingomer get old enough to stand sentry?"

Heloise laughed. "Last winter, Papa. You wrote the scroll, remember?"

"How did I get so damned old?" Samson grumbled.

The sun was just beginning its slow journey behind the treetops as the Tinkers' house came into view. A long, low passageway linked the house and the even larger workshop, its slate roof exceeded only by the steeple of the Emperor's shrine just off the village common. A large opening at the peak vented black smoke, and Heloise felt the heat long before she reached the huge double doors.

Samson tried the great bronze ring, pulling until he grunted. He looked up at Heloise, embarrassed. "Locked?"

"Not locked," Heloise said, taking hold of the ring. "You just have to lift first, and then they swing right open." The thick wood creaked as the door swung wide.

"I suppose I shouldn't be surprised. You and Basina Tinker are attached at the hip."

The heat of the workshop hit Heloise like a wall, a thick dampness that had her sweating before she drew breath.

Barnard Tinker stood talking to Sald Grower, while Sigir, the Maior of Hammersdown, impatiently waited for the tinker's attention. Barnard was nearly twice the size of Sald, his tan skin stretched over a mountain range of muscle, marked by the burn scars common to all tinkers. His two sons, Guntar and Gunnar, were smaller versions of their father, with bronzed skin and powerful shoulders. They followed their father's example of shaving their heads, which glistened with sweat. They offered Heloise only a short glance before turning back to their work.

Basina Tinker was the mirror of her brothers, save that she kept her hair, a nod to her inevitable duties as wife and mother. She was like Austre, older and taller than Heloise, and more womanly, save the strong muscles of her arms and the bronze luster of her skin. She smiled as Heloise appeared and Heloise thought she had never seen anyone so beautiful in all her life.

Sigir was thick and tall like Samson, with darker hair and softer hands, a thick moustache that hung to his chest. His chain of office was polished to a high shine.

The fruits of the family labor were scattered all around, plow blades and cistern pipes, wheel rims and pry bars. Metal reflected the light cast by the molten glow of the crucible that dominated the workshop's far end, the huge cauldron bubbling with molten iron.

The light from the crucible played around a plain bronze door, set into the thick pitch-soaked logs of the workshop's wall. Behind it lay the Tinkers' vault, where they stored their Imperial commissions, secret and safe.

"Sigir, I'm glad you're here . . ." Samson began.

"Whatever it is will keep for a moment," Sigir said. "I've been waiting here since—"

"Stumps need hauling, Master Maior, won't be another moment." Sald brushed his hair from his eyes and gave a short bow to Heloise. "Miss Factor."

Heloise curtsied.

"Sacred Throne," Barnard said, "the whole village is in my

workshop today. Everyone mind themselves while I get Sald settled."

Barnard led Sald to the workshop's side door. A pair of oxen stood outside, one of Barnard's tinker-made yokes over their shoulders. Long metal rods extended from the yoke, running down the creatures' legs to leather straps at their ankles. Barnard turned to the great pile of seethestone stacked beside the door, bundled in salted cheesecloth to keep it dry. He took up a knife from one of the worktables and cut off a small piece and some of the cheesecloth, wrapping it carefully and passing it to Sald. "Keep that dry. Even a drop of water will have it boiling."

Sald held the seethestone as if it were a poisonous snake. Barnard grinned as he handed him a mug of water. "You don't have to be frightened of it, Master Grower. Keeping it dry will suffice."

Sald nodded, and moved to the tiny metal canister on the top of the yoke. "Seethestone's already in there," Barnard said. "Put the stuff I just gave you in your pocket, in case you run out before the job's done. Just add the water."

Sald looked doubtfully at Barnard as he opened the canister. He held the mug over it, hesitated. Barnard rolled his eyes. "It's not wizardry, Sald. Just dump it in."

Sald emptied the mug into the canister. Heloise heard the seethestone sizzling at the water's touch, could smell the high, acrid tang of the smoke that came wafting out. Sald jumped back, and Barnard reached across, slapping the canister lid shut. "Once you wet it, you don't want to let any out. Don't forget that if you have to charge it again. And don't touch it when it's wet. It'll burn you worse than boiling water."

Sald raced to gather up the oxen's steering lines where they lay coiled at the team's side, as the pipes running from the canister began to rattle. "Not much to remember," Barnard said. "If the engine dies, just put in the rest of the stone and wet it again. A single mug will do."

Sald nodded. "You're sure you won't take coin . . ."

"Not from you," Barnard said, gesturing to a big, ancient-looking tree stump squatting near the workshop wall. Long chains were already lashed to it, trailing back to the oxen's harness. "Have the yoke back by nightfall. You should be able to pull all the stumps you like with that engine on your team."

"I'll take care of your stump," Sald said, "and I'll bring you a sack of cabbages when I bring the yoke back. It's mighty generous of you, Master Tinker."

"All our riches come from the Emperor." Barnard waved. "We must not be miserly with them."

Sald nodded, flicked the leads, and clucked the oxen into motion. The stump was enormous, and the taproot must have been deep within the earth, but the rods on the tinker-yoke pushed in perfect time with the animals' footsteps, and it came dragging out of the ground with a sound like a great ripping of cloth.

The oxen lurched forward, unused to the power in the tinker-yoke. They stumbled, found their feet, and the stump bounced along the track back toward Sald Grower's patch.

"Pulling a stump and a sack of cabbages?" Samson asked. "That's all the rent you'll charge for a day's use of a tinker-engine?"

Barnard shrugged. "Cheaper than having to keep my own team of oxen. Besides, Sald's a neighbor and a friend."

"You can throw a stone from one end of Lutet to the other. Everyone's a neighbor and a friend."

Barnard shrugged again. "The Emperor is my judge."

"Not sure he's going to think you a better man for giving away your shirt. Though if I had that sweet honey from the Emperor's own purse, I suppose I could afford to be more generous too." He jerked his chin at the sealed vault door. "Is that why the Order is about? Are they picking up one of their commissions?"

Barnard shook his head. "If they were, I'd have told you already. You think I'd leave a friend in doubt?"

"The Order's about?" Sigir asked.

"Aye," Samson replied. "That's why I've come. We met them on the road to Hammersdown."

"Do you still want to talk business?" Barnard asked Sigir, but the Maior ignored him, eyes locked on Samson.

Heloise knew she should listen to her father and the Maior talk. The Order being nearby was important, and the Maior might have questions for her. But Basina made it all seem less important somehow. Heloise smiled shyly at her, and Basina grinned back, the crucible's light playing on the muscles of her arms.

"What are you working on?" Heloise asked.

"My groom gift." Basina snatched up a rough metal armlet, still glowing cherry red from the forge fires. The ends were caked with ash, but Heloise could see the skilled twists in the metal, the grinning faces that marked the ends. "Randal said he doesn't want anything too splendid."

Heloise didn't like being reminded of Basina's betrothal. Basina married would mean she would be gone to her husband's house, and an end to their nights whispering secrets by the fire, or days gathering wood together.

"You met the Order?" Sigir asked.

"They rode past us on their way to Frogfork," Samson said.

"Then why do you look so worried? Maior Annalee's got a good head on her shoulders. She'll give them whatever plunder they're bent on this time and then they'll be on their way."

"Churic's lost his head."

"He was born with a lost head." Barnard shrugged.

"He was raving about being a wizard. Said he had the portal

in his eye. Shouted it so loud, I'm surprised the Order didn't hear it in Frogfork."

Sigir and Barnard's expressions froze. "Are you certain?"

Samson nodded. "Heloise was with me. I told them to turn Churic out."

Sigir looked to Barnard. "Foolish words are the only things that travel faster than horses. They will know, and soon."

"Don't borrow trouble, Maior," Barnard said. "When the Order knows, we'll know. Jaran's no fool. He'll find a way to keep Churic quiet."

"In the meantime," Sigir said, "I'll double the watch."

"If the Order comes here," Samson said, "the watch will do us precious little."

"Is it true?" Basina asked Heloise.

"It is," Heloise said. "They had a Sojourner leading them. He called Papa a liar and I . . . I talked back to him."

Basina caught her breath. "Oh, Heloise. That was very stupid."

Heloise grinned, proud of the awe she saw in Basina's eyes. "I know. It was, but you should have seen him! He didn't know what to do!"

Basina laughed and Samson turned to them. "That's enough. Basina's right, Heloise, it was very stupid."

"You were lucky," Sigir said, frowning.

"We were." Samson agreed. "They had two dead in tow."

"Did you recognize them?"

Samson shook his head. "The road had had its way with them. Wasn't enough left to recognize."

"Come on, Heloise," Basina said, setting down her hammer. "Let's go down to the well, and you can tell me about it."

"Oh, no you don't," Barnard scolded. "You owe me work until supper, as we agreed."

"Fine, Father." Basina rolled her eyes, and Heloise felt a stab of disappointment.

"Please, Master Tinker?" Heloise asked him. "I haven't seen her all day."

"You see plenty of one another," Barnard said. "Basina's a groom gift to finish, and I want the rough work done by tonight. Besides, I don't think your father is feeling terribly indulgent after you tweaked a Sojourner's nose."

"She's brave, I'll give her that," Samson said.

"Brave and young," the Maior said.

"Brave and stupid," Guntar groused from his workbench, then ducked his head as his father threw a brass mug at him.

"Shut your hole," Barnard growled.

"Best you head home," Sigir said to Samson. "Leuba will be wondering where you've gone to. I'll send word on the sentries. I suppose all we can do now is watch and wait."

Heloise gave Basina a hug, kissed her cheek. "I'll miss you!"

"I'll miss you too. Maybe I can convince Father to let us see one another after supper. I'll work as fast as I can."

"I'll wait by the well," Heloise whispered in her ear. "See if you can get away to draw water or something."

Basina smiled at her as they turned to go.

Heloise paused by the common well on the way home, careful to seem pensive and worried.

"Come on, dove," Samson said. "Your father's no great harbor from a wicked world, but there's more comfort to be found hearthside. Your mother's soup and the sight of home will do you good."

"What if the Order is coming here?"

"Then the sentries will give us warning long before they arrive, and we will be ready."

"Ready for what? To run? To fight?"

"That will be for the Maior to decide."

"Can I sit for moment? By myself? Just trying to take joy in the day, Papa, as you told me to."

Samson blinked up at the sky, looked back down to her, eyes sad. "I'm sorry you had to see such things, Heloise. I would spare you the world if I could. That'll be your husband's task someday, and he'll likely fail at it just as miserably as I have. But your mother's done all right. Women are tougher than they look."

She hugged him around his big belly. "We are. I'll come in at the gloaming, I promise. I just . . . I want to be outside now."

Samson kissed the top of her head and smiled. "At the gloaming now. Don't want the Kipti stealing you away."

Heloise rolled her eyes. "That's just a story, Papa. The Kipti don't really steal children."

"Still, don't make me worry." He turned and walked off toward home, glancing at her over his shoulder as he went.

Heloise sat and watched the wind toss the trees at the common's edge, but her mind was again full with the image of the dead woman's face, her body coiled in chains and her own guts, sliding down the road. She tried to think of something else. A husband, being betrothed like Austre or Basina. Heloise would go to live in her husband's house, to honor his father and mother, to tend to his trade. But when she closed her eyes and tried to imagine life as a wife, she saw nothing, only an empty space dragging out before her. *It's because of the shock you've had,* Heloise thought. *Try and think of the life you'd want.*

The only image that came to mind was a day in the past spring when Barnard had made Basina and her a little kite with a tinker-engine to help it fly, puffing seethestone smoke as the wind filled the cloth and pulled it to the end of its string, and Heloise had only to run and look at Basina's eyes and her smiling mouth. It had been warm, and chores were done and Heloise had thought she could run like that forever.

The thought made the sour feeling in her stomach ebb, so she returned to it again and again, and before she knew it, the wind had picked up and the sentries changed again, and the light began to fail. The gloaming had snuck up on her, and her father would be furious if she wasn't home soon. At least the Order had not come, but Basina hadn't either, and Heloise swallowed her disappointment.

Heloise ran for her house, so intent on beating the failing light that she blundered into a pair of legs as solid and hard as oak trunks. She stumbled back, went down hard.

The legs were clad in coarse gray wool, shot through with leaves and twigs. A rotten-looking leather pouch hung at the waist, along with a hatchet, head up so that the keen edge could be clearly seen, the only part perfectly clean, glowing with a fresh coat of oil.

The voice that boomed from atop the legs gave the lie to the hard appearance. It was soft and kind. "Where are we off to in such a hurry?"

The man bent at the waist, bringing the rest of him into view. The coarse wool leggings matched his shirt, and a leather pack slung over one shoulder matched his pouch. But there, the hardness ended. His face was warm and open. His wide black eyes danced, the corners crinkling. He reached out a long and gangly arm, offering fingers as knotted and cured as dried leather.

"Clodio!" Heloise scrambled up, letting the old man draw her to her feet and into a tight embrace, her head resting on his chest, smelling of old leather and leaf mold.

"Well, now," Clodio said, his hard hand gentle on the back of her hair. "Aren't you a little wood tick today? It can't be an old man's soft clothes that has you so tucked in."

He gently pried her loose and pushed her back. "What's eating you, girl?"

Heloise thought of telling him about the Order. Clodio's dark eyes seemed to talk to her, speaking more clearly than words. *Life is a joy*, they said. *The world is wide and wonderful, and I am glad you are in it.*

She couldn't bear to see that humor fade, to have it replaced with concern or, worse, sympathy. She was so glad to think of something other than the dead woman and the chains and the Order.

She shook her head. "What did you bring?"

Worry bent the corners of Clodio's laughing eyes. He knew she was avoiding the question, but he wouldn't pry. She loved him for it.

"What makes you think I brought anything?" He asked, hands falling protectively to the leather pouch at his waist.

"You always bring something," she said, reaching for it. She meant something other than what he had to sell. Clodio was a wanderer and a finder of things. This sort of bushpig quill that the jeweler needed for a necklace. That special mushroom, that crushed up in broth would break a child's fever. Shells and stones and once even a box of tiny metal balls for the Tinkers, fetched all the way from the Far Tygres where men walked on their hands, if Clodio was to be believed.

"Well, that doesn't mean I brought anything this time," the old man said, spinning away from her. "At least, nothing that's of interest to little girls."

"I'm not a little girl," she said, keenly aware of how her giggling made her sound like one. "I'm almost a woman grown and betrothed, and I want to see what you brought."

"What I've brought for sale, or what I've brought for you?"

"You always bring me a present."

"You're almost a woman grown and betrothed, you just said. Too old to be chasing my hems for presents."

Clodio spun away from her, faster and faster, reaching out one long arm to keep her at bay, Heloise chasing and laughing.

"You," the old man breathed, "are the slowest little girl I have ever met."

Heloise chased twice as hard, her laughter coming in great hiccups. They spun faster and faster, until he suddenly stopped and she collided with his bony hip, bouncing off and going down on her backside again.

"Ow," she said. "That wasn't . . ."

But Clodio wasn't laughing anymore. He was straightening up, smoothing the front of his filthy clothes.

Samson made his way toward them, his mouth set in a hard line.

"Master Factor." Clodio tugged his forelock, bowing slightly from the waist.

"I'm no lord," Samson said, waving the gesture away. "Leave your courtesies for such men as have earned them. Tell me instead why you're playing round-the-mulberry-bush with my little girl."

Clodio frowned. "Just a game, Master. No harm in it."

"Papa . . ." Heloise got to her feet in a rush.

Samson stopped her with a gesture. "I'll not have you chasing the hem of a bush ranger," Samson said, "and you said you'd be home by gloaming, which in case you'd not noticed, is upon us. I'm surprised at you. You're nearly a woman grown, Heloise."

Heloise opened her mouth to say something, but Clodio touched her elbow. "There, now. Your father is looking after you, as it should be."

Heloise swallowed, looked down at her feet and did her best to look sorry. Samson straightened, his expression softening, but he did not smile as he unfolded his arms. "The Order is about."

"I know," Clodio said. "I've come by way of Hammersdown."

"They're wizard hunting. They were dragging villagers behind them."

"I know that, too."

"Do you know who they were?"

"Not yet. Out of Silverbrook, most likely. A man and a woman."

"They said they were bound for Frogfork. Do you know if that's true?"

Clodio shook his head, glanced at Heloise. "Best taken up with the Maior, I'd think."

There was a long silence, and Heloise waited, hoping that one of them would say more, but all her father said was, "Well, what has your ranging brought this time?"

Clodio smiled again. He opened the pouch. "You'd asked for bloodvein."

"You found it?" Samson asked, his expression lightening. Heloise brightened as well, leaning forward. Bloodvein's deep orange color turned red when mixed with water. Ground in oil, the stone produced the precious red ink their clients liked for their signatures, and for which Samson could charge double the fee per letter.

"No"—Clodio's smile didn't waver—"but this is heartfruit rind." He produced a handful of scraps of what looked like dried meat. The faint light brown color did not look promising.

Samson looked at Clodio's open hand doubtfully. "What is this?"

"It is a delicacy of the desert Algalifes. Their champions quest for it in the height of summer, losing their lives for the chance to bring back but one fruited branch from the tree. For such a man may make his fortune."

Samson sighed. "That may be, and I'd still count it worthless if it can't color ink."

Clodio laughed and moved to clap Samson's shoulder, saw the

man's hard face, thought better of it. "It does as well as blood-vein," he said. "Note the name. This is the heartfruit. Don't let its skin blind you to the wealth within."

"A ranger and poet," Samson snorted. "All right, then. Helo-ise, fetch the mortar and pestle and meet us at the well before the light fails." He turned back to Clodio. "If it's as you say, might be there's some coin for you. Then you'll come with me to see Sigir."

"Not coin," Clodio said. "It's a letter I need."

Samson frowned. "Not the same letter."

"The same. Always the same."

Samson's next words were soft, kind. "I'd spare you this chain, Clodio. Take coin. Leave off letters that will never be read."

Clodio's eyes went dead. The ranger's voice was low, dry sticks rattling over sand. "Ranger I may be, but I'm man enough to have my letter without your gainsay."

Samson looked angry, but Heloise could tell when her father's anger masked fear. He threw up his hands. "Fool enough, you mean." He turned to Heloise. "Did I not tell you to fetch grind-ing kit?"

Heloise nodded and ran for the house while her father and Clodio made for the well, arguing.

Leuba sat just inside the door. Heloise's mother was a gray lump under her wimple, her small mouth working silently in time with the clicking of her knitting needles. Heloise knew her mother well enough to guess those silent words were prayers to the Emperor, reciting the Writ over and over, beseeching the Sainted Palantines to protect the family, the village. Heloise felt the same mixed feel-ings she always did at the sight of her mother. Leuba was good and kind, but she was also . . . small, somehow. She cooked, and she cleaned, and she prayed. She never took an interest in the family trade, or the counsels of the men. Heloise knew this was right, how a wife was supposed to behave, but when she thought of that future for herself, it made her feel tired and sad in equal measure. She loved her mother, but her father had fought in a war, and traveled through the valley to ply his trade, and the Maior consulted him on matters of import. She felt a stab of guilt at the thought. Her mother did as the Writ said a mother ought. That should be enough.

Leuba started as Heloise came in. "What's all . . ."

"Clodio's come! He brought heartfruit all the way from the Tygres, and he says it's just as good as bloodvein and . . ."

"Your father's seeing to him?" Her mother's voice was tight.

"Yes. And if you're going to warn me off him, Papa's already told me."

"Mind your tongue. What's got you in such a rush?"

Heloise was grateful to talk of something other than the Order. "Father says I'm to bring his grinding kit to the well. We're going to see the color of the ranger's wares. Come on, Mama!"

Leuba swatted Heloise's backside, pushing her into the house. "Well, you'd best be quick about it. Hurry along and get him his things."

The main room of the Factors' house was bare and black from the hearth smoke, the only decoration a bright silver statue set atop a thick beam and surrounded by long dead flowers that Heloise was supposed to have kept fresh. The statue showed one of the nine Palantines, devil-slayers, saints who, unaided, managed to kill the spawn of hell before dying of their wounds. The Palantine was shown with his arm extended, palm outward, forbidding the devils to cross the veil into the world of men. Heloise knew the statue should make her feel safe, but it didn't. Even if a Palantine had killed a devil, none of them had survived the fight. To meet a devil was to die.

Beside him, just visible from the floor, were the family's Knitting

MYKE COLE

staves. One for each man or woman grown, as was required by the Writ. They had never been moved in as long as Heloise could remember, and a thick layer of dust covered them.

Heloise snatched her father's mortar and pestle off the table, paused. "Mama?"

Leuba had set down her needles and was striping a dried chicken carcass, crumbling the pieces into a pot of boiling water. "Mm-hm?"

"Clodio wants payment in letters, Papa tried to get him to take coin. He won't."

Leuba looked up sharply, was silent for a long time. "Your father only wants to help him. Clodio is chasing something he lost, and it isn't good for him."

Heloise frowned. "What is he chasing?"

She expected her mother to dismiss the question, shoo her out the door. But Leuba was only quiet again. "Sometimes," she finally said, "you can love something too much. So much that trying to love it starts to hurt you. Think of your heart getting too big for your body to hold."

Heloise tried to imagine loving someone so much that it hurt her, but the only person she could think of was Basina, and the thought of something as good as that friendship causing her pain didn't make sense.

"What do you mean?" she asked.

Leuba sighed. "Enough of it. Leave the poor man alone. Bring your father his kit so we can get Clodio paid in the manner he chooses."

Heloise ran outside. Samson and Clodio were standing to either side of the well, talking in the low voice they saved for when they recounted the war.

"No, I haven't seen him for at least a year's span," Clodio was saying. "He went farther and farther each year, and each time when he came back he was . . . less somehow. A man can lose his grip on the world, can drift beyond it."

"Wizardry," her father said, and spat.

"No," Clodio said. "Nothing like that. He just . . . you see terrible things in war."

"I know," Samson said. "I was there beside you. Put my pike between you and Ludhuige's own shield bearer, if memory serves." He glanced sideways at Heloise, as if he would have said more if she'd not arrived. "I've seen all you have, and done my duty regardless."

Clodio shrugged. "You're a strong one, Samson. Not every man is so blessed."

"My strength is the Emperor and His Holy Writ."

"Aren't you pious for one who is so green at the sight of the Order?"

"The Emperor is divine. The Order are just men. You don't fault a whole faith just because some of its agents take to brigandage. My faith kept me through the war, and it hasn't failed me after."

Clodio smiled, tapped the hatchet at his hip. "Seem to remember I had a hand in that as well."

Samson shrugged. "All things serve the Emperor. This isn't talk for a young lady, give the kit here, girl."

Heloise handed over the mortar and pestle, standing on tiptoe to peer over her father's elbow as he filled the bottom of the bowl with water from the well bucket, dropped in one of Clodio's rinds, and set to grinding.

A moment later he dipped his finger in the paste and held it up, admiring the thick orange coating the tip. He grunted. "It's not bloodvein, but I won't deny it's got worth. How much have you got?"

"This is just a sample. I've got more cached at my camp."

"How long are you here this time, Clodio?" Heloise asked.

"The roundhouse was empty," the old man answered. "My bedroll's there until another ranger shoves me off. I've custom enough to keep me at least a fortnight. I'll see you again."

"Not at the roundhouse, you won't," Samson groused. "Heloise's got no business in abandoned towers."

The sentry horn sounded. "'Ware riders!" came Corbus Tanner's voice from the tower. "Riders on the southern road! Coming hard!"

Clodio did not hesitate. He bent, squeezed Heloise's shoulder and raced for the woods on the far side of town.

"You'd best be away," Samson said, "the Order's no friend to rangers. If it's them, you'll want to be gone when . . ."

He turned, saw that Clodio, quick as a deer, was already lost in the graying thickness of the distant trees.

"Well," Samson said, "he's no fool."

Samson turned back to the tower, cupped a hand over his mouth. "Brigands? What do you see, Master Tanner?"

"Gray cloaks!" Corbus shouted back. "Flails!"

3

INSOLENCE

They held the gates of their enemies,
Save the Emperor and His nine,
The Sainted Palantines, mortal men, who alone and
  unaided,
Brought the devil low, and each was grievously wounded,
So that they died, and could not rejoice in their victory.
  —Writ. Cas. IV. 24

Heloise stifled the urge to reach for her father's hand again. She'd been brave in the face of a Sojourner today. She could be brave again.

Samson cursed, cupped his hand again. "How many?"

"Hard to tell . . ." Corbus shouted back. "All of them, I think."

"Come down from there, you damned fool. Stow the spear under the tower. No sense in giving them cause for offense."

"And what if we need it?" Corbus panted as he raced down the ladder.

"Against the Order?" Samson asked. "Pray that we don't."

He turned, snatching Heloise's elbow and leading her back toward the house as feet pounded toward them. Sigir came first. He carried a tipstaff and his kind eyes were wide and frightened. Barnard was beside him, and Poch Drover and some of the other village men and their wives came running from their cooking fires. Leuba appeared around the side of their house, chicken carcass still in her hands.

"Well, it seems the village has come to me," Samson said, stopping.

"Is it the Order?" Sigir panted.

"It is," Samson said. "Hard riding by the sound of it."

Corbus appeared from under the tower, paused to strip off his helmet, throwing it back into the darkness and smoothing out his thinning hair. "What do we do, Maior?"

Basina pushed past Barnard and ran to Heloise, taking her arm and pulling her close. Heloise felt safer and stronger with Basina at her side. She scanned the crowd, taking in Barnard's sons who had come to stand behind their father, all three Tinker men carrying their heavy forge hammers, huge things that she doubted most men would have the strength to swing. Barnard's wife, Chunsia, appeared behind them, tiny compared to her giant husband and sons, her hair loose around her shoulders. She'd had no time to don her wimple at the horn's call.

Sigir exchanged glances with Barnard and Samson, cast his eyes over the growing crowd of villagers arriving each moment. "Well, everyone's turned out, it seems," he said, tossing his tipstaff under the tower. "I suppose we should prepare the expected welcome. Best not court a fight if there's none brewing."

"They were wizard hunting," Samson said doubtfully. "I told you what . . . what I saw on the road."

"They were wizard hunting in Frogfork," Sigir answered, motioning to the Tinkers, who nodded and added their hammers to the growing pile, "and maybe Hammersdown, but most likely not. They could be coming for supply."

"At a gallop?" Corbus asked.

"A man can ride fast for many reasons," Sigir answered. "It's not a call to draw swords."

"Bad choices," Barnard spat.

"It's always bad choices. That's why I'm the Maior, to save your tender hearts the burden of making them. Weapons under the tower. Now."

Heloise and Basina clung closer to one another as staves and pitchforks clattered onto the growing pile. "Stupid to throw the weapons away," Basina whispered to her. "If there's to be a fight, we'll wish we had them."

Heloise looked at Basina's strong arms and shoulders, smaller than her brothers' by half, but still bigger around than any village girl's and certainly Heloise's. She pictured Basina fighting to defend her, felt her heart race at the thought. "Sigir says there's not to be any fight."

Basina nodded. "Emperor grant us that he's right."

"Knees!" Sigir called as hoofbeats sounded and Heloise saw the black shapes of riders moving through the darkness.

Heloise felt her heart race, her blood pounding in her veins as she dropped to her knees, dragging Basina down next to her. It was the second time she'd knelt before Pilgrims that day. The mud was just as cold.

In moments, a forest of horse legs surrounded them, and she could smell their lathered hides and hear the creaking of their leather harness. She kept her eyes down, but she was careful to count the legs. There were at least ten Pilgrims, maybe more. The horses circled, whinnying nervously, before their leader reined his mount in and leapt off to the ground, spattering mud on Sigir's legs. Heloise looked up at the bright blue of his eyes and recognized him. He was the Pilgrim from the road, the one who had called her father a liar. Anger kindled in her belly, rose slowly into her chest.

"Welcome to Lutet, Holy Brother," Sigir said. "We are blessed to have the Emperor's Own with us as the day wanes."

"It is fitting that we come with the night," the Pilgrim said. Heloise looked up at him, then. He didn't look much older than Basina's brothers, though it was hard to tell if he'd a man's shoulders because of the armor. Armor made everyone look like giants. Heloise could hear the hardened leather pieces scraping against one another as he brought his flail off his shoulder and thumped it into the mud, his blue eyes blazing. "For we have dark work before us."

"If any can hold back the darkness, you can, Holy Brother," Sigir said.

The Pilgrim nodded. "I am Brother Tone, Hand of the Emperor. You are the Maior of this settlement?"

"I am, Holy Brother. I am called Sigir."

Tone's ice blue eyes narrowed. "What was your trade and name before you were raised up?"

"Potter, sir."

"Potter . . . I do not know the name. Are all assembled?"

Sigir didn't bother to look around. "They are, Holy Brother."

The Sojourner turned to take in the crowd. He took a long time of it, looking over everyone while the Pilgrims sat silently behind him, the only sounds the wind sighing in the trees and the horses tugging at their reins as they tried to crop the short, stubborn grass.

"Subjects of the Emperor!" Tone's voice was high and thin, but it carried to all. Troupers had come to the village when Heloise was little, and put on a show in the common. They'd had voices like that.

"It is good to see you here, in proper obedience to the Emperor. It is good to treat His Writ with gravity. It is this which assures His blessing. It is this which keeps His eyes turned toward you.

It is through the Emperor's valor that we are made safe, that the worlds are kept apart. It is through His vigilance alone that the devils are kept from our door. What is the Emperor's first command?"

The words came bubbling to the lips of everyone on the common. "Suffer no wizard to live."

"Suffer no wizard to live," Tone repeated. "A simple law. And all the Emperor asks.

"If your father, your son, or your brother is a wizard."

"Cry out to the Order," the village spoke with one voice.

"If your mother, your daughter, your sister."

"Cry out to the Order."

"And the Order shall answer, always. And how shall you secure the Empire until the Order arrives?"

"Stone them."

"You know the words, but do you live them?"

Silence at that. Heloise felt sick with fear. She could sense that Tone was coming to his point.

"Soft hearts may wish to save a beloved friend, a sweetheart, a cousin"—Tone leaned forward, the flail's chain jingling, and lowered his voice to a whisper—"and damn all mankind.

"I can see!" Tone said. "I can look in a man's eye and see the gateway there. I can smell the stink of wizardry like others smell sulfur. And I have smelled it! Two we found on the road and put to the question, two criminals who would have sold us poisoned fodder in the hope of slowing our sacred charge. They died hard, all the harder for having the Emperor's benevolent eye turned away from them. But before their souls passed into hell, the Emperor breathed upon them and found the tiny grain of truth that remained. They told us what we needed to know."

Heloise pictured the bodies in their chain wrappings sliding along behind the Pilgrims' horses. She looked up now, heedless, half-expecting the Pilgrims to dismount and begin swinging their wicked-looking flails among the crowd.

But Tone only folded his arms across his chest. "The veil is rent. The blight is in the valley, on your very doorstep."

A chorus of gasps from all the villagers, muttered cries of "No," and "Throne protect us."

Sigir stumbled to his feet, "Holy Brother, are you certain that . . ."

"You are rising to do your Emperor's bidding!" Tone took a step back from the Maior. "That is good. All shall rise and make ready. What is rent, must be Knit. Now is your time to stand in the line, to fill your duties as the Writ has laid them down for you."

Tone glanced sidelong at the pile of shadows under the sentry tower, smiled. "I see you have gathered weapons in anticipation of your duty, and that is to be commended. But you will be a Knitting line, not a levy. You will not need them."

Sigir looked as if he might weep. Heloise's heart twisted at the sight of his thick moustache trembling, his normally steady eyes flitting back and forth, like an animal looking for an escape. "Holy Brother . . . are you sure this is . . ."

"Needed?" asked Tone. "Perhaps I am not sure. Perhaps I should ask for the counsel of an upjumped potter. Or a wheelwright. Are there any goatherds in your number who would care to counsel the Emperor's Own as to how best to keep the realm safe from hell's reach?"

Sigir's face darkened, but he looked at his feet. "My apologies, Holy Brother. I spoke out of turn."

Tone stabbed a gloved finger at him, the flail head jerking, setting the chain jangling again. "Not at all, Master Potter. There's no harm in questions. Perhaps I am wrong. Perhaps we should ride on. Perhaps we should leave the blight to spread, until wizardry makes its home in your own benighted hamlet. Perhaps you would prefer we all turn from the hard work of keeping the veil shut, until the rent appears here, and you stand on the wrong side of a Knitting line yourselves. Is that what you want?"

Heloise could see Samson and Barnard's faces darken. They were veterans of the Old War, and Barnard's sons glanced at their father's expression, setting their own to match. Basina even tensed at the threat, letting go of Heloise's arm and squaring her shoulders.

But there were ten Pilgrims, all armed and armored, and who knew how many more were in the column Heloise had seen on the road? Fifty? One hundred?

And more importantly this: The Order was the Hand of the Emperor. To defy them was to invite the wrath of the Throne itself.

"No, Holy Brother," Sigir said.

"I thought not," Brother Tone said. "You have a drover?"

"I am the drover," Poch Drover said, stepping forward, "and I've two boys who know the trade . . . if it pleases you, Holy Brother."

"The Emperor provides," Tone said. "It falls to you to cart the people. I will leave a rider to guide you.

"There is another matter. The light of the Sacred Throne flies before us, chasing the shadows out of the corners of the valley. We fear one of those shadows may have fallen on your own village. A ranger. A wanderer whose name is written on no village roll, who casts off the Emperor's protection, trusting to his own power. This is pride, and no mistake, for when a man thinks himself the Emperor's equal, the gateway to hell opens a crack to receive him. We would speak with him, give him the chance to repent of his ways and return to the village rolls."

Heloise swallowed. She flicked her eyes to her father, but his face showed nothing. Clodio was as swift as a deer, as clever as a cat. The Order would never find him.

"Come," Tone spoke into the silence. "He's been here. Do you expect me to believe that a ranger came past your doorstep and didn't stop for trade? If I look through your larders, will I find freshly sharpened knives? Will I see new pots? Spices in your evening stew?"

"You might see sharp knives, Holy Brother," Barnard said. "I'm a tinker."

"And I don't need to remind you who your tinkering serves first and foremost. You have an Imperial vault in your shop, I should hope."

"I do."

"Then I trust you are hard at work at whatever the Imperial Procurer has tasked you to, and that when we come to collect it, it will be ready."

Barnard bowed slightly. Heloise had never seen him so angry.

"Now, the ranger! Where is he?" Tone's eyes swept the villagers.

No one answered. Heloise felt the words creeping up the back of her throat. Who knew what Tone would do if he didn't get the answers he wanted? *Maybe he won't hurt Clodio. Maybe they just want to talk.* But she looked at Tone's armored shoulders, the flail haft gripped tightly in his fist, and she didn't think so.

"This ranger is a heretic!" Tone said. "A man who mates with other men. Like lying with like, like the devils in hell themselves. You would protect him? We will remember it if you tell us, I will report it to the Holy Father, who will look on you with favor."

He stalked among the villagers, looking at their faces, as if he could see the truth there. "Rangers do not plant as the Emperor commanded. They move endlessly, carrying their sin from place to place, seeding blight instead of crops. They are a plague."

Heloise felt the anger rising again, as hot and as quick as on the road to Hammersdown, when the Pilgrim had called her father a liar. She opened her mouth to tell him that he should get out of her village, bit back her words, but not before she had uttered a strangled growl.

Tone's eyes snapped to her, and Heloise drew closer to Basina, as if a little girl could protect her from a Pilgrim. Tone smiled, squatted in the mud, placed the flail crosswise on his thighs. Heloise could feel her father tense, could see Barnard take a heavy step toward them. Heloise should have been comforted by their nearness, but what could they do against armored men with spiked flails?

"So, girl? Do you have something to say?" Tone asked.

The Writ promised dire punishment for liars, so Heloise was careful to tell the truth. "I've got nothing to tell you, I swear."

"You make your oaths to the Emperor, not to me, for it is He who will judge you on the last day if you lie," Tone said. He turned to Basina, and as his eyes fell on her, Heloise felt her legs go weak. "And you do lie, I think," he said. "Well, how about this one? Do you have anything to tell me?"

Basina's cheeks had gone dark. Her eyes shone with tears, her chin quivering.

"There's no need to cry," Tone said, reaching out to brush at her cheek. Heloise knew Basina's tears were born of anger, not fear. "I am only trying to protect you. To protect all of you."

Basina turned her face away, swatted Tone's gauntlet down. "Don't touch me," she snapped.

Startled, Tone rocked back on his haunches, put out a hand to stop himself from falling. "Disobedient . . ." he said, reached for Basina's arm.

Heloise's body betrayed her.

The fear and worry, the thought of the dead woman's face, all disappeared. Now, there was only Tone's arm moving toward Basina, the rest of the world vanishing in a buzzing fog behind it.

"Get away from her!" Heloise shouted, pushing hard on the leather vambrace, sending Tone tipping sideways and going down hard on his backside, mud smearing his gray cloak.

Tone scrambled to his feet, leaning on his flail as he rose. "You little . . ." he snarled, lunging for Heloise.

She shrieked, dancing back a step, and then the heavy bulk of her father was between them, his wide chest against the Pilgrim's breastplate, hands on his flail.

Chains jangled as flails came off shoulders and into ready hands. Horses stomped as the other Pilgrims reined them around, spread out. Heloise could see the crowd tighten, fists bunched, eyes angry. Sigir sidestepped toward the pile of weapons under the tower. Barnard stepped in front of Basina, his two big sons behind him.

"Holy Brother, please," Samson whispered. But while his words were pleading, his face was as savage as a wild dog. His eyes bored into Tone's, the muscles in his shoulders trembling.

Brother Tone's eyes passed over the crowd, and Heloise thought she saw a glimmer of fear there. The Pilgrims had their weapons and armor, but there were at least three adult villagers for each of them, and that didn't count the bigger boys like Ingomer and Barnard's sons. Tone's eyes returned to Samson's and the fear in them grew. He shook the flail haft. "Release it," he said, his voice cracking.

Samson spread his fingers and then his arms, dropping the flail and stepping back.

"I know you," Brother Tone said. "From the road today."

Samson said nothing. Heloise could feel the mood of the crowd, like a pot on the verge of a boil. She knew she should feel afraid, but she only felt angry.

"What is your name?" Tone demanded.

"Samson Factor, Holy Brother," her father lifted his chin.

"I will remember you, Samson Factor," Tone said, his face as savage as her father's.

Then, the savagery melted away into a trouper's smile. "Very well, I believe the girl. There is no ranger here." Tone turned to Sigir. "Gather your people. Have them fetch their staves and follow my rider. The Holy Father himself commands it."

Sigir stared, pale-faced and sweating, for a moment before bowing and knuckling his forehead. "Yes, Holy Brother."

Tone swung back up into the saddle, leaned the flail against his shoulder. The other Pilgrims reined their horses around, dug in spurs, and rode out of the village. Tone hesitated for a moment, pulling back on the reins as his mount pawed the earth, anxious to join the others.

His eyes met Samson's once more, and Heloise could see him marking her father's face, remembering the gray eyes, the thin lips. And then Tone gave the barest nod, hauled the reins back over and dug in his spurs, and suddenly Sigir was shouting for Poch Drover to hitch up his carts and people were running to their homes to fetch their staves and make ready.

Samson put a hand on Heloise's shoulder. "Come on, dove. You're safe now."

Heloise looked up at him, eyes wide, her heart pounding. *What about you, Papa?* she thought as she pictured Tone's hard eyes, marking her father's face before he wheeled his horse away.

What about you?

4

THE KNITTING

Captain-General addressed us today. Said that old Ludhuige's grandfather was a fallen Palantine, and that his blood was tainted. Said it was preordained that Ludhuige would fly the red banner and take up arms against the Emperor. Says it's the same for his bitter and jealous men.

But I've been in this war since it started, come face-to-face with them time and again.

They don't look bitter. They look like me.

—from the journal of Samson Factor

They left the weapons where they lay.

The villagers streamed back to the common, awkwardly shouldering their Knitting staves, each as long as a man was tall, thick around as the haft of the Pilgrim's flail.

With the sky still fading to purple-gray, Poch Drover appeared with his heavy horses in harness, the huge logging cart rolling behind. His eldest son, Char, pulled up alongside in the second cart.

"Right!" Sigir shouted. "In you go! Up, everyone."

Heloise clung to Basina's arm, dragged along in the rush to the side of Poch's cart. She felt her father boost her up, grabbed hold of the rail, and swung herself over, jostled by the other villagers scrambling to find seats. The staves pointed skyward, a forest of headless spears. She reached back down over the railing, touched her father's arm. "Papa. I can't do this."

"Be brave, dove," he said, pulling himself up after her, "and pray to the Throne that it will go lightly."

"But do we have to . . ."

Samson swung a leg over and reached down to help Leuba up. "We do. There's nothing to be gained from fighting the Order, and no winning if we do. We escaped unharmed this time, but they'll be back if we don't move with a quickness, and there will be more of them, and angrier."

"Come, poppet," Barnard called to Basina. "We're in the other cart."

"I want to stay with Heloise!" Basina said. "We'll be right alongside each other."

Heloise nodded so quickly her chin thumped her chest. Barnard looked like he would say something, but at last he kissed his daughter and ran for the other cart. Samson settled on the bench, leaving a spot for Heloise to squeeze in between him and Basina, and the girls clung to one another as the cart got rolling and the village common began to drift away.

Heloise looked up at her father's face. Even in the fading light she could see the creases in his brow, the trembling of his lip. She had never seen him like this before, and it frightened her so deeply that she felt a sudden mad urge to run as fast as she could with no direction or purpose.

"Papa"—she touched his arm—"I'm sorry. I got angry again." The words broke as they came out. It was her fault the Pilgrim had asked her father's name. Her fault that he'd taken the long look at her father's face before he'd ridden away.

But she couldn't let Tone hurt Basina. She would never let anyone hurt Basina. Not if it meant her life.

Samson looked down at her. His brow smoothed and his eyes lost their frightened look. He took a deep breath, and the ones he took after were slower. He looked at her for a long time.

"No, my dove," he said. "I'm not angry with you. It was a foolish thing you did, and dangerous, but I'd have done the same."

"What's going to happen now?"

Samson only shook his head, one ink-stained hand touching his wife's hair.

Heloise looked away from him, saw the boulder atop the Giant's Shoulder growing in the distance. She recognized the road. She had walked it just that morning.

Hammersdown. *Men are soft when it comes to their own.*

"Now you listen well to me, children," Samson said. "Not sure how bad it'll be tonight, but . . . well, we have to be ready in case it is. I've only seen a Knitting once in my life and then when I was a soldier. It's a terrible thing, but you have to remember the need. The veil's all that keeps hell itself from reaching out to snatch us all in."

He looked at his knees, sighed. "More than children should have to see," he said, his hands tightening, "but . . . just remember *why* this thing is done. Remember it and hold it close. The Knitting is what comes of forgetting."

Heloise's stomach suddenly felt dead, a rotting thing stuck in her belly.

She looked back to Basina. The girl had turned white.

The dead woman's face flashed in Heloise's mind.

"It's because of Churic, Papa. That's why this is happening."

Samson sighed. The frightened look had returned. "Maybe so, dove. Maybe so."

"But Papa . . ." Heloise began. "Churic is simple . . . Jaran said he was no wizard."

Samson grabbed Heloise's chin. "Simple or no, Heloise, you'll do what needs to be done. By the Emperor you will obey the Pilgrims. Do you understand me?"

His voice broke at those last words, a tremble in it that Heloise had never heard before. *He's trying not to cry.*

Heloise looked into Samson's eyes and it was as if the fear bled from him and into her. Her knees shook and her chest felt tight. The sky was suddenly heavy, as if the darkening clouds might fall upon her. She couldn't breathe. She was out in the open, how could the world feel so small?

Basina put her arm around Heloise's shoulders, her warm breath against her ear. "Heloise," Basina said. "It's all right. It will all be all right."

And just like that, the world was right sized again. Heloise was still afraid, but the fear was a thing she could endure, like a fever or an aching tooth, awful, but not the killing kind. Heloise put her head against Basina's shoulder and they rode on in silence.

"I'm not brave," Heloise said. "I'm frightened."

"You were very brave back there with the Pilgrim," Basina said. "You protected me."

Heloise surprised herself by laughing. "I've never been so frightened in my life."

Basina flashed her a smile. "Father says being brave isn't not being frightened, it's doing a thing even though you are."

Heloise shut her eyes and inhaled the smell of Basina's skin, pretended that Basina wasn't going to marry Randal, and instead they were promised to one another. She knew the thought was impossible, but it felt right. It helped her to be strong.

After a while, Heloise looked up and saw Brother Tone standing in the road.

Heloise recognized the narrow carter's track that wound its way through the thickness of the forest. Hammersdown was just through the woods beyond.

"I don't see any wizard-blight," Heloise said to Basina. According to the Writ, the woods would be dark and rotten, full of strange sounds, plants and animals twisted by hell's touch.

But it was only normal ground, scattered stones and young trees, just a few years grown back from the last timber harvest.

The Pilgrim raised his hand and the drover reined the horses to a stop.

"Come on!" Tone yelled. "Out! There's not much time."

The villagers came stumbling out of the cart, nearly stepping on one another in their rush to obey. Heloise stood with the children, watching as each adult villager assembled, staves planted in the ground before them. Heloise waited for Tone to speak to her father, her heart pounding, but his eyes passed over Samson as if he were not there.

Heloise saw Barnard helping his wife to the ground.

"Father!" Basina waved.

"Go with your family," Tone said to Basina. "Second cart takes the east side."

"Can she stay with me?" Heloise blurted out. The thought of facing what was coming without her best friend made her stomach clench.

She heard Samson suck in his breath, and the Pilgrim fixed his eyes on Basina. "Go with your family, I won't ask you again."

Basina took Heloise's hand and didn't move.

The Pilgrim's eyes blazed. He turned to Barnard. "Your child is willful. I would whip her if I had time."

He'd said nearly the same thing to Samson when they met on the road to Hammersdown, but Barnard was not her father. The tinker's arm twitched as he took a step forward. "You would . . ."

The Pilgrim let his flail slide into his hand, the iron chain jingling. "One more step and I will make time."

Barnard looked as if he would say more, then he jerked Basina's hand, dragging her away.

"It's all right," Basina called to Heloise as she was towed along behind her father. "You'll be all right!"

Tone nodded in satisfaction, then turned to the assembled villagers. "Attend me! Hold the pole like this," he held his flail crosswise, his arms extended, the shaft resting on his thighs. "Leave a man's span between each of you."

The villagers did as they were ordered, and the Pilgrim walked among them, moving this man here and this woman there, until they stood in a line disappearing into the trees to either side of Heloise. Again, he passed right by her father, and again did nothing more than give Samson a sharp glare.

Heloise stood between her parents as Brother Tone gave a final grunt and pointed into the woods. "There lies Hammersdown. Pious subjects of the Emperor, sheltering beneath the might of His Holy Writ."

The trips between each turning of the moon, her hand in her father's. Hammersdown had been part of her life for as long as she could remember.

"But some among them thought they knew better," the Pilgrim went on. "They thought they could reach beyond the veil and hide it from the Righteous Throne. The Emperor sees all! To His unblinking eye, the wizard is a fire burning in the dark. The Throne's justice is swift, and it is merciless. One of the folk of Hammersdown dabbled in the dark fire, made himself strong beyond the reach of mortal men. He saw the night as if it were day, he ran swift as the deer. He grew younger."

Heloise's stomach turned over. *It's not true*, she wanted to yell, but what good would it do? She felt her useless empty hands, opening and closing on air.

"Hell gave all this to him and more," Brother Tone went on,

"so much that Hammersdown could not fail to see, but they were weak, and frightened, and they did not cry out to us. They waited until the Emperor's gaze fell upon them, and by then His heart was hardened against them."

Heloise could hear distant shouting. Another Pilgrim was giving the same speech further down the line. There were screams of fear and anger deeper in the woods. She smelled smoke.

"By then, the veil was torn," Tone continued. "Had they cried out to us, had they followed the Holy Writ, we might not be here today. But they did not.

"What are the words?"

"Suffer no wizard to live," the villagers said as one.

"And today, all of Hammersdown is wizard-touched. Wizardry is seeped into the stones. The trees drink from it. The birds stretch their wings and course on its currents.

She glanced up at her father. He had said he'd hoped it wouldn't be bad, but this sounded bad. This sounded very bad.

"Now, we Knit the veil!" Tone went on. "Now, we close the fracture that would have the devils walk amongst you once again. Now we scourge the very earth until no shred of the contagion remains.

"Women you will see today, and children. Men weeping. Some you will know. They will cry their innocence. They will beg you to stand aside.

"You will not. No one gets past you. You are the border of the wickedness that plagues this place. It shall not escape, or the Knitting shall expand until it encompasses even your own homes."

Brother Tone turned, looking at each of the younger villagers sprinkled between their parents. "You bear no staves, but do not think that because you are not yet grown that this task does not also fall to you. There are not enough men and women grown to cover all the ground we must. You must be the eyes and ears of your parents. Keep a sharp lookout, and warn them of the approach of the tainted. Do not let them pass."

As Brother Tone's eyes met hers, Heloise's fear grew so intense that she felt as if she were hovering above herself, looking down on a different Heloise. It couldn't be her who was standing in this line, about to help kill people she had known all her life. It was someone else. It had to be someone else.

Shadows moved in the woods behind the Pilgrim. Heloise could see peaks of flame above the trees. She could hear screams coming louder now, felt her skin break out in gooseflesh. The scent of smoke grew stronger, bringing strangely tasty smells. Cooked meat, fish oil. She swallowed back bile. She wished the anger would come now, would give her the strength to defy Brother Tone, but it didn't. There was only the sick fear, making her limbs feel heavy, rooting her to the spot.

"Hold, damn you! For the Emperor!" Brother Tone turned his back, raised his flail, and disappeared into the wood before them.

The villagers stood, eyes straight ahead, waiting. Nothing happened for a long while.

"Papa," Heloise whispered to her father. "Is it going to be bad?"

Samson looked at her, his eyes huge.

There were shouts, the sound of clashing metal, but nothing moved in the wood save the dancing flames, their roar rising until it was nearly as loud as the screams. Then, a scrabbling in the trees. The underbrush shivered, went still, then exploded.

A herding dog ran out of the wood, eyes wide with terror. Its hide smoked, its tail trailed fire. It yipped, whined.

Heloise knew that dog. She had scratched its ears and thrown sticks for it to set at her feet, barking until she threw them again. Alna Shepherd's animal. Callie.

The dog pawed at the ground, long front legs digging in. Callie was a herding dog born and bred, made to run.

She bolted straight toward Heloise before skidding sideways as she saw the other villagers. She paced the line, yelping, turning back and forth, desperate for a way through.

"Get!" Samson shouted, striking at Callie with his staff. The dog flinched, tucking her burning tail between trembling legs.

Heloise realized that she was crying now, felt the hot tears tracking down her cheeks, though she couldn't hear her own weeping over the sound of the roaring flames. The dog turned, faced Heloise's mother, tucked her head. Heloise knew Callie had made her decision.

The dog jerked left, then dove right, racing toward the gap between Heloise and Leuba. Heloise moved toward it, frightened that Brother Tone might see her letting it go, but her heart wasn't in it, and she was much too slow. Leuba cried out, swatting the creature on its fetlocks and falling on her backside. The dog howled and bolted through the line, disappearing into the woods behind them.

No one spoke. All behaved as if the dog had never gotten through, eyes fixed on the wood, straining to see if the Pilgrims had noticed.

A shout sounded in front of Heloise, and a man stepped out from between the trees. His head dipped inward, like an egg that had been dropped on its side. Blood coursed from the wound, bits of yellow and gray flowing into his beard. Alna Shepherd, looking for his dog.

His eye was gone. His speech slurred as her father's did when he'd drunk too much beer. "You killed us!" he shouted. "You bastards. You killed us."

The words fell on Heloise like a hammer. *It wasn't us*, she wanted to shout. *It was Churic. Papa told you to put him out.*

Alna lifted a short bow, the string long since snapped, and aimed it at Heloise. He tried to pull the broken string, stared in confusion at his hand passing through air. "Done nothing," he whispered, drooling. "Killed us."

And then Brother Tone was behind him, flail moving through the air, the black spikes crashing into Alna's head, sending him toppling sideways, the light going out of his remaining eye. The iron stuck in his skull, and the Pilgrim put one boot on the man's back, worked his arms to pull it free. It came away with a wet slurp, spraying blood.

Heloise watched the red droplets race toward her, saw the solid pieces in the mist, shut her eyes. *Oh, no. Please no.*

She felt the hot touch as it splattered across her face, the pieces sliding down her neck behind her dress. She cried out, fell to her knees, her stomach lurching.

Someone called her name, her father maybe. She looked up to find the sound, saw Brother Tone standing over Alna, his flail rising and falling, rising and falling, as steady as her father chopping wood, bringing it down into the red-gray mush that no longer looked like a man.

Heloise could hear herself screaming, as if the voice came from a long way off, another girl just like her. She tried to remember her father's words. It was necessary. The veil must be shut.

But she looked at the man slowly pounded into the mud, at the Pilgrim's burning eyes, his teeth bared, bent on the completion of his task. Chopping wood. Pounding dough.

This wasn't right. This couldn't be right.

More screams. A girl ran from the woods, coming straight toward her. She wasn't much older than Heloise, her dark hair full of leaves and blood, mud on her face. Her dress was torn away, and she clutched the ragged remains to cover her nakedness. Heloise barely recognized her. It was Austre. Austre who had played with her when she was little. Austre who was going to learn letters from her. Austre who had promised to show her her betrothal dress. Her throat and thighs were bruised, her new breasts poorly covered by one flailing arm.

Another Pilgrim was hard on her heels. His hood was back, his eyes lit with the same hunger she'd seen before in men. He was a heavy man, in armor meant for riding, and he ran slow and clumsy until at last he stumbled and fell on his face.

"Stop her!" Brother Tone shouted. He struck out with his flail, missing her by a hair's breadth.

Austre pounded toward Heloise, closer and closer. Heloise knew she was supposed to get to her feet, trip her, something. *No, this is wrong.* Heloise knew it would mean her life to help Austre, but she wasn't sure she could do otherwise. She tried to stand, but the horror unfolding in her gut made it impossible. She fell forward, vomiting in the dirt.

Heloise turned, saw her father twitch toward Austre, but his eyes filled with tears and he didn't move further.

Austre vaulted over Heloise's head, and the Pilgrim followed. Heloise fell in her own sick, sprawled on her side. "No," she tried to say, only mumbled.

Austre dashed up the path, nearly as fast as Callie. Brother Tone's voice was lost in the screaming and the roaring fire. Heloise wondered if her father would move to help now, or her mother, but no one did. Brother Tone's boots let him run over the rocks and roots, but he was older and heavier, and the girl wasn't wearing armor or carrying a heavy flail. As Heloise got back to her knees, the space between the girl and the Pilgrim widened.

"Go," Heloise whispered. "Run."

Austre ran, letting her torn dress fall. Brother Tone was panting now, big shoulders heaving. He swung his flail, cutting air behind her.

Then Austre's foot came down on a stone, turned sideways, her tiny ankle taking all her weight. She shouted, fell.

Tone reached her in three steps, bringing his iron-shod boot down on her back, raising the flail's long shaft and bringing the spiked head swinging into the air over them. Austre lay face down, pale and still, as if she were already dead.

Heloise didn't scream this time. She had no screaming left in her. The sickness was a low buzz in her belly. Her arms and legs felt weak and heavy. She closed her eyes, but it didn't stop her ears, which heard the wet crunch as the Pilgrim brought the flail down again, and again, and again.

There was silence, then. The crackle of the flames behind Heloise were almost soothing, warming her shoulders, the back of her neck.

Crunching of boots, a shadow falling on her. "You let her go."

Heloise opened her eyes. Brother Tone's cloak was soaked with gore, the wet fabric sinking into the gaps between his pauldrons and breastplate. His hood had fallen back, his face covered in blood, so that he looked made of red, save the bright blue of his eyes.

This is what a devil looks like, Heloise thought. *This is what you see before they take you.*

"You let her go," Brother Tone said again, and now Heloise realized that he was speaking to her father at last. Tone shifted the flail from his shoulder into his hands, swinging the head. "I see the portal in your eye now. You are a gateway to hell. Wizard-tainted. You betrayed the Emperor."

And then, in barely more than a whisper, "And you don't have your village mob to help you now."

He's going to kill my father.

She could hear her heart beating, a slow pounding in her ears in time with her breathing, as loud and close as the bellows in Barnard's workshop. The Pilgrim's flail swept before him as he raised the shaft.

Sounds loud in her ears. Her mother shrieking. Her father shouting, "She was just a little girl." She could hear Brother Tone's boots hitting on the ground as he raced for her father. *Don't hurt my papa,* she thought. But she couldn't speak. Couldn't move. Now, when she needed her anger most, it would not come.

She heard the crash of wood against wood over her head as two shafts met, the sound jolting her onto her backside. Her father and Brother Tone snarled at one another, knuckles white on their lengths of wood. Heloise fumbled with her fingers, scrabbling over the roots and rocks, heedless of the thick wetness that covered everything.

"You, dare!" Tone hissed at her father, pressing the flail haft in and down, trying to free the spiked head enough to swing it at him.

Heloise's hand closed on a loose rock. It was small, a skipping-stone really, not big enough to hurt anyone. She choked back tears for a battle cry and brought it down on the top of Brother Tone's boot. The leather was so hard that she might as well have struck iron, but Tone cursed and looked down, eyes leaving Samson's for just a moment.

And then Brother Tone was falling back, reaching out with the flail to stop himself from landing on his back.

Her father followed him. The bristle on his face was gray, and his stomach hung over his belt, but his shoulders were wide and his eyes clear. He held his staff like a pike, thrusting to catch the Pilgrim as he tried to get his balance. The pole struck Tone's cheek loud enough for Heloise to hear. The gray cloak tangled the Pilgrim's arm and Tone stumbled back, finally stopping his fall with the flail. A dark bruise was already showing on his face, blood trickling from the corner of his mouth.

Heloise's father came after him, trying to keep him off-balance, but the Pilgrim had his wind now, and knocked the pole aside.

Samson rocked back on his heels and slid smoothly into a wide stance, holding the pole over his head, pointing at the Pilgrim. "You killed a little girl, you bastard."

Tone looked at Samson's stance. "You're a veteran, aren't you?"

"Come on, damn you," her father said.

The Pilgrim smiled, a white line across his red face. "This isn't the Old War, and that's not a pike." He spun the flail's head.

"And he's not alone," Sigir said, stepping out of the line, holding his pole just like her father.

Brother Tone looked left and right. He was wearing armor, and his spiked flail looked a lot stronger than the wooden poles. "So be it," he said, smiling.

"Aye," Barnard said, stepping out of the line, raising his own pole. "So be it, Pilgrim, and may the Sacred Throne bear witness."

Brother Tone's eyes widened, then narrowed. He walked backward, ignoring Barnard and Sigir, looking at the man who had given him the bruise.

"I'll be back for you," he said to Samson, then turned and disappeared into the wood.

5

WE DIDN'T HAVE TO DO IT

Column marched over the Castle Rock yesterday and took up the King's Highway. Came across a Kipti band living in their wagons.

They sharpened our pike heads for us, and mended cartwheels. Good job of it, too. They say every Kipti is at least half-tinker.

The levy Pilgrim was furious that we gave custom to heretics, but that didn't scare the Captain. "Writ won't fix our wheels," he said, "nor make our weapons sharp."

Saw the Pilgrim later, when he thought no one was looking, having one of the heretics mend a locket some sweetheart had given him.

—from the journal of Samson Factor

The sun was beginning to rise when another Pilgrim stumbled wearily out of the drifting smoke and dismissed them with a wave.

No more people were driven their way. There was a scream here and there, but most of the night was spent standing in silence, squinting through the drifting ash and boiling smoke.

They climbed back into the cart, exhausted, eyes down. It was silent for the jostling ride back, the same look on every face. Exhaustion, mostly, but also something that looked like shame. No one spoke of the dog who had escaped, or of the girl who hadn't.

Samson's brow was furrowed, his cheeks purple. He didn't talk about his fight with Brother Tone, and Heloise knew it would be unwise to bring it up. Heloise wanted to shout at them all, at herself. *This is our fault. We did this.*

"Had to be done," Samson said. "I told Jaran to shut that simpleton up."

Heloise didn't realize he was speaking to her until Leuba put a hand on his shoulder. "Husband—"

"It had to be done," Samson repeated, cutting her off. "You have to remember that. A Knitting is a terrible thing, but the devils are worse. The Emperor did it for us once, now it's for us to do it for ourselves. That's our strength, His gift to us."

It didn't feel like a gift. *Churic was simple. He wasn't a wizard.*

"If even one had gotten through"—Samson tapped Heloise's knee—"it could have been worse."

Then what about Callie? Heloise thought. Her father was lying, not just to her, but to himself. Worst of all, he expected her to repeat the lies, to act as though up was down of her own free will. It was a stupid, wicked way to live, and the smoke still smudging the darkening sky showed how it ended.

"Had to be done," her father said, straightening and looking away. But the words had an upward lilt at the end, like he was asking a question.

At last, the cart rocked to a stop, and Heloise looked up to see them back on the village common. Her arms and legs felt like they'd been filled with metal. She sat as the cart slowly emptied, her parents slumping to the ground. Samson turned back to Heloise. "Come on, girl." Heloise wasn't ready to move yet, her mind still whirling.

"Leave her." Sigir's voice. "I'll send her along in a moment."

Heloise heard her father hesitate, then grunt assent. Her parents' steps dwindled in the distance, and still Heloise sat, feeling the cart rock as the people left, until suddenly it was still, and she knew she was alone.

"Come on, child," Sigir said from the ground beside her. The grief in his tone was honest, and it gave her the strength to stand.

The Maior looked tiny from his place beside the cart, as thin as the poles they'd carried, his ash-streaked face shadowed by the growing darkness, eyes bruised-looking from exhaustion. He held up a skinny hand. "Come down, now. It's over."

"Papa says we had to do it," Heloise said. "He says if we hadn't, the devils would have come."

Sigir said nothing as she took his hand and jumped down to the ground. She looked up at him, saw the horror on his face, the deep lines the day's events had cut in him.

"Did we have to do it?" she asked.

"No," he answered, his voice breaking, tears falling into his beard to turn the flakes of ash to gray slush. "No, child. We didn't."

Heloise thought she should feel angry at his words, but when she searched her heart, she could only find fatigue. "Then why did we?"

"Because they would have killed us if we refused," he answered. "Because it would have been our village, our fields, our families they Knit."

"Why us? If they're so worried about wizard-blight, they can use the army."

Sigir shook his head. "The army has other tasks. Old Ludhuige may be rotting in his grave, but his generals still fly the red banners. This work falls to the Order."

He took a deep breath, then spoke again. "And making us complicit means we will never call them to account for the crime."

"But what if we fought them? Papa hit that Pilgrim in the face and . . ." *And I hit him in the boot with a stone, though no one saw.*

"Your father is very brave and he loves you very much. I pray that he will not be made to pay for that. It is one thing for a man to fight another man, it is another for a village of men to try to stop the might of the Order."

"But we have tipstaffs and the Tinkers have weap—"

He covered her mouth with his hand, not roughly, just enough to stop her speaking. His palm smelled like smoke and burned meat. "We have both spoken heresy today. That's a dangerous thing, Heloise. I'll answer your question, and then we'll speak no more of this, and you have to promise me that you'll remember that while your thoughts are your own, the words you let past your lips belong to the world, and the world will not always take the meaning you intended."

She nodded.

"Most men in this village fought against Ludhuige in the Old War. I knew your father then. He was a brave man, and strong. He would fight like a lion to protect his home and hearth.

"But war also taught me odds. How many men and how many swords you need, how much time must be spent in the drill yard learning to hold a line, to shore pikes and stand against a charge.

"We would lose, Heloise. We would lose quickly and utterly and the wages would be just as bad as a Knitting. Maybe worse. We are farmers and smiths and wheelwrights. The Order speaks of ministry, but it is the paint over the board. The wood beneath is killing. It is what they train to do, it is what they are equipped to do, it is all they do."

They stood in silence for a moment, Sigir slowly mastering his tears. At last he brushed a lock of her hair back behind her ear and sighed. "I am sorry, Heloise. The world is not as I would have it. Go tell your father to come to me. We must decide what to do now."

Heloise turned to go, but Sigir called her back. "Remember never to speak of what was said here tonight. The pious might take it amiss, and we will have trouble enough with what your father has done."

He left her, then, and the world that had been so full of smoke and flame and screaming was replaced by the last shreds of cool night, stars beginning to fade as the sun banished the moon, the soft, warm glow of the hearth coals dancing in the windows of her home.

"Heloise!" Her father, his voice rising. "Come now, girl."

She ran to her father. Once again, he was in danger because of her. He should be angry.

But he wasn't. He caught her around the shoulders as she came through the door, pulling her in. She tensed, expecting a scolding, but instead felt the soft surface of her mother's bosom, her father's hand on her back. She blinked, realization dawning. He was holding them. Heloise could feel his breath coming in short gasps. *He's trying not to cry.* The thought terrified her.

"It's all right, Papa," Heloise said. "It's all right."

"It's not all right. My little girl." Samson sighed. "It will never be all right."

He held them for another moment, then stood away, an arm on each of their shoulders. "You are dear to me, the both of you. You should remember that."

Leuba nodded silently. After a moment, Heloise did the same.

"It's over," he said, though he looked like the one who needed comforting. "It's over now."

"Not my first Knitting," Leuba said. "We're alive and we're together, and that's what matters."

They were silent for a while after that, and then Samson shook his head and took his wife's hand. "Aye, wife. It's so. We'll speak no more of it."

"The Maior wants to see you," Heloise said. "He says you have to figure out what to do now that you hit that Pilgrim."

The kindness winked out of Samson's face. "I said we'll speak no more of it."

"But Papa, Sigi—"

"Enough!" Her father's cheeks reddened.

"Samson." Leuba laid her hand on his arm. "They will come for you. You must flee."

"Flee where, woman? I am a factor, not a trapper. I cannot feed myself in the wild with winter coming on. And if I do escape? What then? Where will I go? Who would take me in with the Order set against me? Who will give me custom? I would be a beggar."

Leuba took a deep breath, spoke slowly. "Better a living beggar than a dead factor."

"The Factors have lived in this village since before the veil was shut. This is my home."

"Samson," Leuba said. "You must . . ."

The door banged open.

"What are you still doing here?" Sigir said through clenched teeth, storming in. "They are coming for you!"

"You come into my hou—" Samson began.

"Spare me," Sigir cut him off. "You have to go. You have to go right now."

Samson repeated the same argument he'd given Heloise and her mother.

"I'll not argue with a fool. I'm the Maior and you are now an exile. Pack a ruck and leave. I'll send the Tipstaff in an hour. If you're still about, he'll beat you blue."

Samson nearly turned blue himself. "I'll damn well do for him like I did for that Pilgrim, and then you'll have a dead Tipstaff *and* me still at home."

"Think of your family!" Sigir shouted.

"I *am* thinking of my family!" Samson answered. "What will they do? You said it's to be a lean winter. Who will feed them?"

"Someone will . . ." Sigir began.

"*Who?*" Samson waved his hands. "Maybe for the first month, but what about the second? And the third? Who will guard them if the brigands come again? And what's to become of me with no trade to ply and no place to go? I'm more dead gone away than I am if I stay. If I'm to die, I'll do it at my own hearthside."

Sigir opened his mouth to speak, shut it. For a moment the Maior struggled, jaw straining. At long last, he sighed. "Come to the gathering hall, then. Barnard saw the fight, and who knows who else. We'll have to parlay on it. There'll be some for putting you to flight, no doubt."

"The Emperor is my judge," Samson said.

"And the Order are His Hands in this world. In case you hadn't noticed, they have judged you unfavorably."

Samson nodded, then turned and placed his hands on Heloise's shoulders. "Run to the Tinkers and fetch Barnard to the gathering hall. It's after dark, so straight there and then straight home to your mother, mind me."

"Master Maior," Heloise said to Sigir, tears pricking at the corners of her eyes. "Will you turn Papa out? Can't you just tell everyone to make him stay?" Heloise felt like she was two people at the same time. One Heloise saw the foolishness in her words, the great risk her father took, not only for himself, but for the entire village. But that Heloise was trampled by another, louder Heloise, who desperately wanted her father to stay, wanted everything to go back to how it was before they had met the Order on the road.

Sigir shook his head sadly. "I am a Maior, not a lord. I will speak for your father, but I am but the loudest voice among many. Do as your father says and fetch Barnard. We don't have much time."

"Run along, dove," Samson said. "It will be all right. You'll see."

"I'm coming with you," Leuba said.

"You know full well that the gathering hall is no place for wives," Samson said.

"I'll not have this be the last time I see you," Leuba said again, balling her fists. "I'll stand at your side and the town fathers will have to look me in the eye as they speak their piece. Might be that will make them think kinder of what they say."

"It won't help," Samson said.

"He's right," Sigir agreed. "Stay here and wait for Heloise. Children are not allowed at parlay either, and you can't have an unmarried girl of sixteen winters at home alone."

"If it's exile—" Leuba began.

"If it's exile," Sigir interrupted her, "I will let you have your farewell, and you can tan the hides of the town fathers beside your husband before he goes." He reached out and touched her wrist. "We have been friends and neighbors since we were children, ma'am. Trust that I labor in your defense, always."

Leuba's cheeks were red and her hands shook, but she nodded. "Very well. May the Sainted Palantines watch over you, husband. May you stand in the shadow of the Throne."

"I always stand in the shadow of the Throne," Samson said, and turned to go.

Heloise stood frozen to the spot, until her mother swatted her backside hard enough to get her moving. "Go on! Run as fast as you can and fetch Barnard!"

Though she had gone a night without sleep, Heloise ran faster than she had ever run in her life. Even with dawn coming on, the sun was still not high enough to light the world, and the common green was a blurring gray plain beneath her pounding heels. Heloise was never let out on her own this early, and in happier times, she would have thrilled at the sudden freedom.

But these were not happier times, and she thought only of her father's fate, her stomach hurting and her breath burning as she burst into the Tinkers' workshop to find Barnard before one of his anvils, hammering away at a piece of metal, cherry-red going to slate-gray under the blows. Basina stood beside him, holding the metal steady with a pair of black iron tongs.

Heloise stopped short. The Tinkers hadn't slept all night either. Whatever she'd expected to find, it wasn't this. "You're working."

Barnard didn't look surprised to see her. "It helps me think. It gives me peace."

"Sig—"

"Sigir wants to see me," Barnard finished for her, "about your father."

Heloise choked back tears. "Will you speak for him, Master Tinker?"

Barnard set the hammer and metal on the anvil and swept her into a tight embrace. "Always, Heloise. Always."

And then he was moving, his long strides carrying him to the workshop door as fast as she could run. "They're at the gathering hall!" She shouted after him.

"I know," Barnard said without turning, and vanished into the gray dawn.

Heloise felt Basina's presence before her arms slid around her, hugging her from behind. Her tow-colored hair brushed across her shoulder, and the smell of it kept the tears at bay. "It'll be all right, Heloise," Basina said. "It'll be all right."

Heloise cried then, great hiccuping gasps, her fingers digging into Basina's arms, leaning her head back to rest on her best friend's shoulder. "I don't want them to send him away."

"I know," Basina said, "but no one has sent him anywhere yet. You can stay here if you like, or I can walk you home."

Heloise's grief curdled to sudden anger. This was wrong. She couldn't go home. Couldn't go sit by the hearth with her mother and wait to hear what the town fathers decided. Basina had been brave enough to stand up to Brother Tone. Heloise could go to the gathering hall in her own village. "I want to go and see."

Basina went stiff, but when Heloise broke free of her embrace and turned around, she was smiling.

"Please, Basina. If I go home, I'll go mad. I'm going to go and listen, and I don't want to go alone."

Basina only nodded.

And they were off and running again, Heloise's terror tipping over into a slanted, twisted joy, so that she wanted to laugh as she had when they ran beneath the kite Barnard had made them. She kept silent, though, so as not to be heard by the men inside the hall.

6

TURN HIM OUT

Then the Emperor set them in the places they should
dwell.
But there were those who were proud saying, "Who art
thou to fix our dwelling place?"
And they forsook the village rolls, and made their homes
on their feet, or in their carts.
The Emperor cursed them, and named them Kipti, and
turned from them.
—Writ. Ala. I. 29

The gathering hall's steep wooden-shingled roof was warming beneath the rising sun, burning off the shreds of the wicked night. Barrach Builder had sheeted the eaves in copper, chased with scenes showing the Sainted Palantines battling devils as the Holy Emperor looked on, His divine presence giving them strength. The light slid over the depressions in the metal, making the Palantines' armor glow.

The men were inside, in such a hurry that they'd left the huge iron-bound doors open, and Heloise and Basina slowed, stepping quietly up to the mortared stone walls. The rock was blessedly cool after the long run, and Heloise took a moment to lean against it, catching her breath and looking across at Basina. Her body cried out for sleep, but she wasn't going anywhere until she knew her father's fate. Basina's face was serious, but her eyes were lit from the run and the knowledge that their parents would be furious if they were caught.

Then Heloise heard her father's voice, echoing through the long hall. "Just listen! Let me finish!"

There were murmurs, and finally Sigir shouting at them to be silent in the Emperor's name. Samson spoke into the silence. "I have known most of you since we were children. I soldiered beside Sigir, and Barnard. And you, Danad Clothier. Poch Drover, I picked you up by your trews and dragged you into the breach in the seawall at Haraven—"

"You didn't drag m—" Poch began.

"I did and half the damn levy saw me do it, and may the Emperor judge you for a liar when you stand in the shadow of the Throne."

Poch began again and Barnard growled for him to shut up. "Samson has the right of it."

"You, Sald Grower," Samson said, "I taught you to keep a book for the Emperor's tax collector. You'd be in a debtor's prison if not for me."

"Aye," Sald said quietly. "What's that to do with this? It doesn't change that the Order will come here for you, Samson, and they'll take vengeance if they find you here."

"It means that you should hear me," Samson said, "and think carefully before you put me out. We don't know what the Order will do if they find me here. Might be that Brother Tone is shamed by losing a fight to a mere villager. Might be he'll tell his brothers that he fell or ran into a tree in his haste to work the Emperor's will. Might be the Order has pressing business elsewhere."

"Might be you're a damned fool," Poch Drover said. "Might be we'll all burn because you're too much the coward to do what's best for everyone."

"If I stay," Samson said, his words slow and his voice even, "I have a chance. My wife and daughter have a chance. We can live. If you turn me out, I will die and my family will be beggared."

"You might live," Sald said. "You don't know . . ."

"I am no ranger!" Samson roared. "This isn't Lyse where I can beg on a corner for the kindness of strangers. I will starve, or I will be taken by wolves and brigands."

As she heard her father's words, Heloise felt her breath stop in her throat. If he stayed, her father would fall to the Order. If he went, he would fall to the wilderness. Either way she would lose him. The world suddenly felt very small again, and she longed to run to Basina's arms, but it was as it had been when Austre had run toward her. Her body refused to obey. Her vision grayed, and she gasped, desperately swallowing air. That made the color come back into her sight, and the men couldn't have heard her over the noise of them all shouting at once until the Maior's voice won out over them all.

"Shut it!" Sigir shouted.

The voices gradually went silent, Poch's trailing last, muttering complaints. "We clearly have no agreement," Sigir said more quietly. "And we know that means the decision rests with me."

"That's not—" Poch began.

"That's the law," Sigir interrupted him. "You made me the Maior. If we are at odds, it is my voice that carries."

There was quiet then, and Heloise stood completely still, not daring to breathe for fear of what his next words would be. It seemed to her that even the wind was still, waiting for the Maior's decision. She felt Basina take her hand, squeezed it so hard that the bones ground together. She knew she was probably hurting her, but couldn't stop herself. Basina only squeezed her hand back, kissed her forehead, waited.

"He stays," Sigir said, and then Basina was holding her up, for Heloise's knees had turned to water.

"Sacred Throne, you've killed us all," Poch cursed.

"We will hide them," Sigir said.

"Them?" Sald asked.

"Leuba and Heloise as well. All three in different places. They must not be together until we know the Order has ridden on and is gone from the valley."

"You'll save his family at the cost of all of ours," muttered someone, but Heloise didn't recognize the voice.

Poch shouted agreement, then asked, "And when they come asking after them? What then?"

"Then we will tell them that Samson fled into the wood, and took his family with him," Barnard said, "and we will all swear an oath in the shadow of the Throne to say that's what happened."

"Even if they put us to the question?" Sald asked, his voice trembling.

"Of course, you great clod," Barnard answered. "There's no need for an oath if they're just going to ask us nicely."

"They'll not put men to the question for nothing," Sigir said. "It's a likely story, and what most would do. They'll believe it."

"They'll know!" Sald shouted.

"They won't," Sigir said. "They'll see the lie in your eyes as fear of them. I've seen this before with lords and men of privilege. And either way, Samson is right. He'll die out there. I know I'd be dead and buried back in the Old War and so would most of you if it hadn't been for him. We do for him and his family, and those bastards can shove their flails up their asses business end first. They've killed the folk of Hammersdown, and I won't promise you that they won't come for us next, but I'll be a devil myself before

I let them kill our hearts. This is my word and it is final, by the authority vested in me as the Maior. I am the Emperor's Hand in Lutet. Samson stays."

There was a short silence at that, followed by murmurs of "Yes, Maior," and "Aye, Maior."

A shuddering breath from Samson. "Thank you."

"And lest any of you consider treachery, remember this. The Order may come, but eventually they will go. Samson and I will be here forever, as will Barnard, and our cousins and children. And we will not forget the man who turns traitor and surrenders his own to ravagers. Am I plain?"

"You are plain," the men said.

"Who will hide them?" Poch asked. "If it's as you say, the flail will fall hardest on them if they're discovered."

"I'll take Samson," Sigir said. "If it's my word that carries today, then I should take the greatest share of the risk."

"I'll take Heloise," Barnard said. "She and Basina are practically sisters anyway. It's the closest to home she could be."

"Aye, that's best. We'll send Leuba to Deuteria. Best not to have a woman grown hiding in a man's house."

Deuteria was the village herber, living alone out in the barrens beyond the sentry tower. She tended a small garden there, and gave counsel to some of the wives when they'd a problem needing women's wisdom.

The men muttered assent, and Heloise heard the voices coming closer, moving toward the doors. Heloise realized she was crying, cuffed at the tears as Basina dragged her around the building's side. There was more talk, but the voices were too muted by the stone for the girls to hear. A moment later, the men emerged blinking into the rising sun. "To your homes," Sigir said. "Tell all that Samson and his family have fled. The less who know the truth, the better."

There was the shuffling of feet as the men set off, but they stopped at a word from the Maior. "I don't need to remind you of the risk we are taking today. The greatest danger lies in weak hearts and turned coats. I need you all to remember the oath you just swore. You will not cry to the Order for mercy. Say it now, while you look me in the eyes."

"We swear it," a chorus of voices responded.

"Even you, Poch Drover?" Barnard asked.

Heloise bit her knuckle as the silence that followed stretched. "Aye," Poch said at last. "Even me."

And then the men were shuffling out the door.

Basina and Heloise tensed to run around behind the hall if Sigir and Samson came any closer, but they heard no footsteps, only Samson letting out a breath that sounded like he'd been holding it for a while. "You know that Sald and Poch were only the ones who spoke against me, but most agreed with them."

Sigir sighed. "I know it. You've really put your fist in the hive this time, Master Factor."

"He killed a little girl," Samson said, his voice hard. "Would you have done any different?"

"No," Sigir said, "but I'd have made damn sure that I killed him."

Samson laughed, though Heloise didn't see what was funny. "Aye, maybe you would have. Only, think kindly of me until the Order actually comes. Poch's no fortune-teller. He may well be wrong."

"For all our sakes, I hope he is. Barnard is with us, and that's the important thing. He's a mountain, that one. Men are right to fear his wrath."

"Aye," Samson agreed.

"They may try to unseat me, Samson. Call for a new Maior."

"They'd have to send to Lyse for an observer. It would take time."

"Aye," Sigir said, "it would. Hopefully enough time."

They were quiet for a moment then, until Samson asked, "Why did you do it, then? Why not turn me out?"

"You think I don't want to? It's not just because you saved me in the Old War, Samson. Truth is that there are no heroes in a pike block. We stand and fall together. We saved one another."

"Then why speak for me?"

"Because I am not like these Pilgrims with pious words in my mouth and murder in my heart. Because putting you out would kill me just as surely as it would kill you. Because unlike the Order I believe in the Writ."

"That you should fall that your brother may stand."

"Aye," Sigir said. "I didn't stand against old Ludhuige's knights because I wanted to live. I stood because I wanted you to live. And Clodio. And Barnard. And every man who came to arms in the levy. That will never change. Not while I draw breath."

"You have the heart of a Palantine," Samson said.

"And the bladder of an old man. Go home, Samson. Tell your family to make ready. I'll come collect you after I've had a piss."

Heloise heard the crunching of her father's boots as he turned for home. "Go," Basina whispered. "If you run fast enough, you can beat him there."

Heloise kissed her and squeezed her arm. "Thank you."

"Go!" Basina said, pushing her.

Heloise ran as fast as she could for the second time that morning, racing through the woods that ringed the common, outpacing her father easily. She would still arrive just moments before him, and out of breath at that. He would know, but she felt she had to at least try. Her feet scarcely touched the ground the whole way. Her father would be staying, and he had told Sigir that Poch's dire prediction might not come to pass. She believed him. She had to believe him.

Even better, she would hide with the Tinkers. Basina would be with her, and they could spend their nights trading secrets by the hearth's light. Out from under her parents' thumb, surrounded by the marvels of Barnard's workshop, her parents alive and well. It wouldn't be so bad. A part of her was even excited for it all to begin.

She'd thought her father had ambled slowly, but when she emerged from the woods by the well outside her front door, Samson was in sight, hands thrust into the pockets of his breeches, walking toward her. Heloise desperately tried to slow her breathing, to wipe the sweat from her forehead, but it was no use. Samson had to see that she'd just arrived and had come running hard.

Her father only ruffled her hair, ignoring the sweat on her forehead. "You're a good girl, Heloise. This next bit may be hard on you."

7

LODGING

Three manners of men, the Emperor decreed:
The villager, who toils for the good of all, bearing the
name of his trade,
The soldier, who fights for the protection of all, bearing
the name of his regiment,
And the Order above all, My Own, My Hand in this
world, bearing no name but Mine own.
—Writ. Lea. XIV. 1

Barnard and Chunsia met Heloise at the door, grave-faced and silent. They gathered the family together in the workshop, with Bolt and Blade, Barnard's two hounds, sitting attentively beside their master, as if they were part of the meeting as well.

"You all well know the gravity of this," Barnard said. "The Order may come looking for her, and it's up to all of us to make sure that we don't give them any reason to expect she's here."

"I promise I won't be any trouble," Heloise said. "I can sleep here in the workshop, and Basina and I can . . ."

Barnard shook his head. "You can't sleep in the workshop, or anywhere else you might be seen. Hiding you means hiding you. We will bring you meals and let you out for a short while and only then at night. It will be hard for you, Heloise, but you must remember it is the only way to keep you safe."

Heloise's stomach fell. This wasn't what she expected at all. "Where will you hide me?"

Guntar jerked his chin toward the vault door, looking askance at his father.

"Aye," Barnard said. "The vault is sacrosanct. Only the Imperial Procurer can order it opened. It will be blasphemy to let her see inside, but I suppose we're well beyond that now."

Heloise looked at the heavy bronze door, imagined the tight, airless space behind it. Her hands shook. "I have to stay in there?"

"We will be just outside, child," Chunsia said. "We'll look in on you as much as we can."

Heloise felt tears prick at the corners of her eyes. "Will it be for a long time?"

Barnard smiled. "I hope not, Heloise. We will see what comes of your father's defiance. I know it is frightening, but you must remember we are doing it to protect you. As soon as it's safe, we will let you out. I swear it in the shadow of the Throne."

Basina put an arm around Heloise's shoulders. "I'll come in to talk to you, Heloise. Can't I sleep in there with her, Papa?"

"No." Barnard shook his head. "If the Order comes calling, they will want to know where my children are. I cannot say you are in the vault. There's no good reason for a young girl to be in there."

Heloise did cry now, though quietly. She felt like a diseased creature, separated from those she loved the most for fear of infecting them. "I'm sorry," she said between sobs. "I don't mean to be ungrateful."

"I know you don't, child," Chunsia said.

"Come." Barnard stood and took a great iron key from his belt.

"Might be you'll think more of your quarters once you've had a look at them."

"Now or never."

"I'm afraid so, Heloise," Barnard said. "There's no telling when the Order will come. We've already delayed too long." The iron key fit into a hole in the plain surface of the bronze. The black metal rattled, but it turned easily, the tumblers sounding with a deep thunk that made the door tremble despite its weight.

Barnard put his hand on the ring. "Stand back now, Heloise. Once it gets moving, it's hard to stop." He hauled on the ring, stepping back as the thick door swung silently open. Musty air billowed out, drying Heloise's throat and making her cough. The vault smelled like a root cellar soaked in oil. Its log walls had been lined with small stones to keep out prying eyes, and it was much colder inside than out.

"We'll give you our thickest blankets," Chunsia said, "and candles."

Heloise realized that she would need to keep the candles lit all day long. The tight space was packed with hungry darkness, as black as the night sky in a storm.

Fear gripped her so tightly that she trembled. The thought of being locked up in that tiny space, alone in the darkness with the smell of earth and metal and oil . . . she started to cry again, turned and hid her face against Basina's shoulder.

"This is where we store our Imperial commissions," Barnard said. "You're the first person other than the Procurer to see it. That's something, eh?"

Heloise knew it was something, indeed. But that did nothing to banish her fear, the tightness in her chest at the thought of all that darkness pressing in on her.

"Come," Barnard said, stepping inside.

Heloise tried to follow, found her legs would not obey her.

Barnard frowned over his shoulder. He had told her there was no time. She imagined the Order riding up the workshop door, shouting in alarm as they saw her. She tried again to step into the darkness, and again she couldn't.

"Come, Heloise," Barnard said. "The only way to weather cold water is to jump right in."

"I can't," Heloise said. "I'm not brave."

"You are the bravest girl I have ever met besides my own daughter," Barnard said. "Come."

Basina's words echoed in her mind. *Father says being brave isn't not being frightened, it's doing a thing even though you are.*

And even though she was frightened, even though a part of her was certain that the moment she stepped past the transom of the bronze door, the cold darkness would swallow her, she took a step and then another, and she was inside.

Barnard was right. It wasn't so bad. Or, at least it was no worse than she'd imagined. The space was cramped, and the smell of rust and old leather so strong it tickled her nostrils. The racks lining the walls were littered with tinker-engines, some nearly as big as her, some as small as a beetle. Many looked unfinished, with rods and pipes sticking out of them at odd angles.

The room was dominated by two engines shaped liked men, hanging from wooden racks in the room's center. One of them was unfinished, its arms stubby and half-formed, one leg missing. The other looked more or less complete. As Heloise's eyes adjusted to the darkness, she saw that they were like suits of armor, giant metal frames articulated with brass rondels to give the rough shape of a man's limbs. Huge gauntlets hung at waist height, permanently clenched into fists. Black slots were cut out of the knuckles, matching the tangs of an arsenal of weapons still half-forged and propped against one of the thick wooden beams that supported the huge slate roof: axes, swords, pike heads.

Helms topped the giant suits of armor, slumped forward, and Heloise thought they looked like ghostly warriors, heads bowed in prayer, floating before her on the thick air.

"What do you think, girl?" Barnard's voice sounded like the metal he worked, dark, deep, booming. "They're coming together nicely, eh?"

Heloise considered the empty machines, eyes roaming the dark space where a man would fit inside. She imagined the thick metal around her. Who knew what great power the tinker mechanisms would give the wearer? "They're . . . scary."

Barnard chuckled, crossed his arms under his broad chest. "To the Emperor's enemies, yes. But the righteous have nothing to fear from them."

Heloise didn't feel frightened now, only curious. "What are they?"

"War-engines. A man inside one of these is as fast as a hound with a scent, as strong as an army, as invulnerable as Sainted Palantines themselves."

"And you built these for the Emperor?"

"I am building them for the Procurer. I am not so high and mighty that he will tell me what he intends them for, but I imagine they will go to the army, yes."

Heloise pictured the giant metal engine sweeping through a levy line, men flying at the touch of its fists. "How do they work?"

Barnard laughed. "Not so frightened now, are you? It's heresy enough letting you in here. I'll not compound it by teaching a child to run a war-machine." He turned back to Chunsia, who passed him a sack of candles. "There's a sparking stone and metal in there to light them," she said, then handed him a platter loaded down with bread and cheese. Barnard smiled and draped a waterskin over Heloise's shoulder. "I locked myself in here accidentally once. I was in here half the day before my boys got me out. You'll have air enough."

The fear returned at the thought of Barnard stepping out, of the great door closing behind him. "Please," she said in spite of herself. "Can Basina stay with me? Just for the beginning?"

"I will, Father," Basina said. "I don't mind."

Barnard exchanged a glance with Basina before sighing. "I am locking a little girl in a dark closet. This monstrous world makes monsters of us all. All right. But only for a quarter candle, mind me. We risk much as it is."

Basina hugged her father, and Heloise felt such relief that she sat down where she was, back leaning up against the war-machine's metal leg.

"You two be careful in there," Barnard said. "No playing around. Touch nothing."

Basina rolled her eyes. "I helped you make half of these."

Barnard laughed at that, and the sound made Heloise easier. "May the Sainted Palantines watch over you both, you jewels, you flowers. I love you."

"Love you, Father!" Basina said, smiling as if being locked in her own vault was as common as breakfast.

Barnard laughed again and the plain bronze door swung shut, slamming home hard enough to make the walls shake, the darkness sending them scrambling for the sack of candles.

8

HOME AWAY FROM HOME

Having set the trades of men, the Emperor ordered their
 houses,
He set the father over his children,
That he may make his trade for the glory of the Throne,
And the wife shall bear him sons, and heed his words, and
 work his will,
As though he were the Emperor himself.
     —Writ. Lea. XIV. 2

The candle guttered like a hearth fire, casting the same orange-tinted shadows along the walls. Basina sat with her, but they didn't tell stories or share secrets. Instead, they held one another and cried out their anguish over what they'd seen outside Hammersdown. To this, Heloise added her fear that the Order would come and take her, or her family, that she would never see her mother and father again, and simply being so tired she could no longer stand it. At last, Heloise had no more tears in her, and she went limp in Basina's arms, not sleeping but not waking either, her eyes fixed on the flickering candle flame.

It felt like just a few moments before Barnard opened the vault door again and Basina stood to go. She gave Heloise a final hug before going to her father. "Will you be all right, Heloise?" he asked. "Do you want for anything?"

Heloise had never felt more alone in her life. She glanced at the food and water, untouched. There were candles enough to last her a day.

Barnard set a chamber pot on the floor, along with a roll of blankets. "We're just outside, remember. If you get frightened, or . . . or if you need anything, just knock on the door. Even if we don't hear, it'll rouse the dogs, and they'll rouse us. If . . . if it's not safe, I'll knock three times. If I do that, you're to be as quiet as a mouse. Not a sound, you hear? If I knock only once, that means I'm coming in. Understand?"

Heloise nodded. "Three times for danger, once means you're coming in."

"Just in case you're using the pot," Barnard smiled, embarrassed. "Anyway, all will be well. Don't be frightened."

"I'm not frightened," Heloise said, though it wasn't true. "Thank you, Master Tinker."

Barnard leaned in and hugged her around the shoulders. "I'll look in on you soon. If the sentries see nothing on the road after sunset, you can walk under the stars for a bit. All right?"

Heloise nodded, swallowing tears. She would be brave. Though the devils themselves should surround her, she would be brave.

"Good girl," Barnard said, and shut the vault door.

And though he had been so kind to her, Heloise felt anger curdling in her belly at those words. She had faced a Sojourner. She had stood in a Knitting line. How could anyone call her a girl anymore?

Heloise thought of lighting another candle, decided against it. Girls were afraid of the dark. She had seen a village burn. She could do without light. She curled up on the blankets instead, exhausted and watching the remaining candle flicker defiance at the darkness. Its wick grew shorter and shorter, until at last the darkness took everything, though whether it was because her eyes had closed or because the candle had gone out, she couldn't tell.

·   ·   ·

Heloise woke in darkness, felt her way to the sack, fumbling the sparkstone and a fresh candle out. She struck the stone against the bit of metal, showering sparks on the oiled wick until the candle finally caught and chased the shadows into the corners. She squatted over the chamber pot before helping herself to some of the food and water. She had no idea how long she had slept, no way to know how much time had passed other than the candle's life. Who knew how long since it had burned out?

She looked around the small room, the chaos and grief of the past day far enough behind her now that she could truly take it in. It no longer seemed so cramped, and there was really no place to hide, which banished fears of monsters hiding in the shadows. She let her eyes range over the metal constructions that lined the racks. Some looked like brass spiders, others like simple scroll-tubes or bowls surrounded by pipes. She couldn't tell what they did, or even where one would add the seethestone and water to make them run.

She stood and looked at the war-machines hanging on their racks in the middle of the room. They looked smaller now, the candle flame reflecting off the brass edging of the rondels, the silver fittings on the pipes that ran the length of the arms and legs. They looked like metal giants whose chests had been flayed open, the space inside big enough to fit a normal man. Heloise remembered Barnard's cautioning words. *Touch nothing.*

For as long as she'd lived, the village folk had whispered of the Tinker vault, told stories of the wonders hidden behind the bronze door. Now that she stood inside it, Heloise was disappointed at how plain it all seemed. Nothing beyond her imagination, just tinker-engines much like the ones she'd seen before. Instead of driving an oxcart, this one drove a man to war, but otherwise it was much the same. Still, she should not touch it.

Heloise sat down and stared, waiting as the time whiled away. She would have to ask Barnard for a copy of the Writ. If she was to sit by herself all day, she should at least have something to do, and meditating on the Writ was supposed to be the best use of idle time. Or maybe her writing kit. She could write a letter to her father. Maybe Barnard could get it to him, or at least to Sigir.

Instead, she stared at the war-machines, feeling strangely like they were people, like she wasn't alone in the vault so long as they were with her. She stood, went to the one that was more complete, letting her fingers run over the leather and metal. Barnard had said she wasn't to touch it, but he only meant it so she wouldn't hurt herself, surely. So long as the weapons weren't attached to the slots in the fist, there was nothing sharp. The machine looked so solid, made mostly of metal, there was nothing a small girl like herself could do to damage it.

She glanced at the bronze door, filled with a weird idea that Barnard could somehow see through it. She had nothing to do. He would understand that.

No, these engines are commissioned for the Emperor. Even entering the vault is blasphemy. But if that were the case, then Barnard had blasphemed by hiding her here, and she had blasphemed by defying the Order. It all made no sense. The world shouldn't be this way. Villages shouldn't be burned because of the ravings of a simpleton. Austre shouldn't be murdered because of where she lived. And Heloise should be allowed to touch a cold, silent metal engine, when she meant no harm, when she was trapped in the darkness, idle and alone. What was one more blasphemy?

She reached up, setting her hands on the war-machine's knees, scrabbling with her toes as she climbed its legs and into the space inside.

It was built for a man grown, and her head came up only into the machine's throat, where a heavy metal gorget kept her from seeing out. She leaned her head back and looked up into the helmet. If she were only a tiny bit taller, she would be able to see. The thick smell of oil and leather made her sneeze, and the sound of her breath echoed back from the metal so close to her face.

She slid her hands into the arms, as if she were putting on a coat. The leather was coarse against her skin, ending at handles above the gauntlets that she could just brush with her fingertips. Buckles and straps hung from the inside of the limbs and the torso, dangling across her, jingling as she wriggled among them. She was kneeling on a leather-covered ledge above the machine's waist, where a man would probably sit. Even if she were sitting on it, she could see her feet wouldn't quite reach the footrests in the machine's legs below her, leather straps on top of what looked like more leather-covered wooden ledges.

It seemed so simple, just like the tinker-yoke she'd seen on the oxen. The rods there had driven the beast's legs, lending strength to its movements. If she could reach the straps, and if the engine was powered with seethestone, this would do the same for her limbs.

She pressed her arm up against the leather and metal armature, grunted as she strained against it. It didn't budge. It was far too heavy to move without the engine running. She looked down at the stack of weapons, the tangs sharp as the blades themselves where they would attach to the machine's huge fists. Maybe in one or two more winters, she'd be big enough to drive it. Brother Tone would not be so high and mighty then, even with a column of Pilgrims at his back.

"Stay away from my father," a voice said. It was a moment be-

fore she realized that it was her own, that she had been so over-
come by the fantasy of driving the machine against the Pilgrims
that she had spoken aloud.

She looked around, embarrassed, but there was no one to hear
her inside the vault. She could see a huge canister over her shoulder, bolted to the machine's back, the piping all converging on
it, as if it were some giant metal spider. *The engine. The seethestone must go in there.* A salted cloth sack hung from a rivet beside a metal funnel that led into the canister. She prodded it, felt
the seethestone inside. The driver would be able to feed the engine without ever leaving the cage. She turned around, slipping
her arms out of the metal sleeves and looking for the lid when a
knock sounded at the bronze door.

She scrambled, turning around again and dropping down onto
the leather-padded ledge. Her legs got tangled in the straps, and she
went off balance, her face slamming painfully against the gorget.
The machine lurched sickeningly. *Sacred Throne, it's going to fall.
They'll find me tangled up in it if I'm not crushed to death.*

She froze, waiting for the mechanism to topple over, but the
wooden rack was big and heavy, and the machine only rocked
gently in place as the tumblers turned and bronze door shuddered.
She scrambled again, desperate to get down before the door was
flung wide and Barnard saw her, but the straps tangled about her
legs, and she was still only halfway to the ground when the door
creaked slowly open and light flooded in, borne on a gust of fresh
air that blew the candle out.

Basina stood in the doorway, panting. "Did it myself," she
grinned as she looked up, leaning against the heavy door. Her eyes
widened as she saw Heloise, and she raced inside, whispering,
"What are you doing? Father will skin you!"

"Please don't tell him," Heloise said. "I only wanted to see, and
I didn't think I could hurt it."

Basina leaned in, her arms still sweating from the effort of opening the door. She untangled the straps, reaching out a hand to help Heloise down. "I won't tell him, but you have to promise not to do it again."

"There's nothing to do in here," Heloise said. "Maybe you could leave me a copy of the Writ? I could study it when I'm not sleeping."

"Are you so pious?" Basina asked.

"No," Heloise admitted, "but I'll go mad otherwise. Do you think you could get my writing kit? I need to spend the time somehow."

Basina nodded. "I know. I'll see if Father will let me come more often. The Emperor is truly watching over you. If my father hadn't sent me to let you out . . ."

"Why are you letting me out?"

"It's after supper, Father checked on you twice before, and you were so tired that you slept right through it," Basina said. "The road's clear. Father says you're to come outside and walk around the house for a bit."

Heloise followed Basina into the workshop, where the Tinkers were working, Barnard and his sons taking turns hammering at a hot piece of iron while the crucible bubbled orange light around them all. After the long dark of the vault, the workshop floor seemed to glow, even though it was dark outside. The air, heavy with ash and smoke, was sweeter than she'd ever tasted, and she stopped and closed her eyes, gulping it down.

"You're all right, Heloise?" Barnard asked, not looking up from his work.

"Yes, Master Tinker," she said. "You're very kind to keep me here."

"Do you want for anything?"

"May I see my papa and mama now? Just for a little while."

Barnard did stop hammering at that, set the heavy tool to rest beside the anvil. "I'm sorry, Heloise. I spoke to Sigir, and while the Order's not on the road here, they're still in the valley and close by. Best to keep you close to your hiding spot in case they arrive. You'll see your parents as soon as it's safe."

"Are they all right?"

"They're fine, Heloise. May the Emperor judge me if I lie."

Her ears believed him, but her heart did not, and Heloise knew that until she saw Samson whole and breathing, she would never be able to know, to truly know, that he lived. She was less frightened for her mother. It was her father the Order wanted. Or would they try to take her as a way to get to him? The thought made her stomach lurch.

"May I . . . may I just be alone for a bit?"

"I'll come with you," Basina began, but Barnard stopped her with a wave.

"Leave her be," Barnard said. "Stick close to the house, Heloise. You can stay out until we get the crucible scraped and put down for the night. Then we'll come and get you."

Heloise turned to go, but Barnard stopped her with a word. "Heloise?"

"Yes, Master Tinker?"

"I can trust you not to go running off, can't I? I know you miss your parents, but there is a time to run and a time to wait, and now is for the waiting."

"You can trust me, Master Tinker."

"I believe I can."

Heloise nodded and stepped out into the cool night air. If the workshop air had seemed sweet, the outside air was even better. She tilted her face up to the stars, feeling some of the worry lift from her. The moonlight washed the pebbles on the path to the common silver. She need only follow it to the green and across it to reach the Maior's house where her father hid. Did the Maior have him in his root cellar? Was Samson even now walking around Sigir's house, looking up at the same stars? Was he worried about her?

She knew she would never make it there and back again in the time it would take the Tinkers to get the crucible scraped, and it would take even longer to get to the herber's to see her mother. The Tinkers would understand, but they would be angry. Worse, she might bring danger to her parents, to all of them. If the Order came and Sigir or Deuteria were suddenly forced to hide her, too, and they were caught, what then?

Besides, whether the Order came or not, she had told Barnard Tinker that she would not go running off, and her father always said a man was nothing without his word. She wasn't a man, but she supposed the point held.

Heloise sighed and walked around the house, keeping close as Barnard had instructed. The wind picked up, setting the treetops to whispering, and Heloise let the sound lull her as she walked, grateful for the feel of her legs stretching, the touch of the cool breeze raising gooseflesh along the backs of her arms.

"Heloise," the trees whispered to her as she rounded the back of the house, wind sighing in the branches. "Heloise."

She froze. Not wind. Not trees.

"Heloise."

She whirled as a figure detached itself from the shadows of the wood, came toward her. "It's all right." The moonlight fell across the figure just as she was about to scream and run, outlining an old man, tall and thin, hard as cured leather. Silver light pooled in the corners of his eyes as they crinkled into a smile. "It's all right, it's me."

"Clodio! How did you find me?"

"Shh. Keep your voice down. I'm not supposed to be here.

Sigir told me to leave the valley, but I had to make sure my favorite factors were all right first."

"Sigir? Have you seen my father?"

"I have. He's well, Heloise. Worried, but well. He told me you'd be here."

"Clodio, the Order came. They're looking for—"

"I know, poppet. I know. Don't you worry. I've made a life staying one step ahead of the Order. They'll not find me unless I want finding."

She raced to him, throwing her arms around him. He smelled of leather and leaf mold, of sweat and hard travel. Of safety and home. "Oh, it's so good to see you, Clodio. Sigir's right that it's not safe for you here, but I'm still glad you came."

"I never got the chance to close the deal with your father," Clodio said, stroking her hair. "Can't go far until things are settled with that."

Heloise hugged him tighter. After all the talk of death and hiding, she was grateful for smaller, safer topics. "You think he'll buy your wares?"

"Your father's satisfied," Clodio said. "He may cross his arms and draw storm clouds on his brow, but the truth is I could sell him his own boots if I'd a mind. He's lucky I owe him for watching my back in the war. He'll take all of the rind and be sending me back to the desert for more, mark me."

"I mark you," Heloise said.

Clodio set a hand on her shoulder. "You must be terrified, Heloise. You put on a very brave face."

She shrugged, "I don't see what else I can do."

"In times like these," Clodio said, "most men and women grown alike act the fool. You're a woman grown, and no mistake. You're sure you are well?"

"Well enough, I suppose."

"You don't sound well, Heloise."

"They are hiding me in the vault, Clodio. It's tiny and dark and there's nothing to do. Basina comes once in a while, but mostly I'm alone."

Clodio smiled sadly. "I wish I could stay with you. I wish I could take you with me, but life on the road is hard."

"The Kipti manage it," Heloise said.

"The Kipti carry their homes on carts. Rangers sleep out under the weather, with the birds and the beasts for company."

Heloise nodded. She hadn't known that she even wanted to go with Clodio until he had raised the possibility, and the refusal now seemed to snatch even that hope away from her.

Clodio slowly opened his pouch, thrusting a hand inside. "I have something for you."

"What is it?"

Clodio drew his hand out of the bag. Nestled in his palm was small gray mouse.

It crouched in his palm as if it were a second home, rubbing its tiny paws together under its twitching pink nose. Its ears were a bit long, its tail a bit short, but otherwise it looked like any of a dozen of the creatures that her mother was forever chasing out of the house.

"I found him foraging in my bags. Each morning, I ran him off. The next morning, there he was again. After a while I just couldn't bring myself to let him go. He's been traveling with me for at least a fortnight now."

"And you're giving him to me?"

Clodio nodded. "To watch over you."

Heloise felt like she was two people at once: the Heloise whose heart was swelling at Clodio's kindness, and the Heloise who was annoyed at being treated like a baby. It was a mouse. It couldn't watch over anyone.

Stop it. Clodio is the kindest person you know besides Basina. He's just being sweet.

Her cheeks burned with shame, and she reached out for the mouse. "I'm living in the vault here, Clodio. I have no way to care for him."

"Oh, he can look after himself. He's an independent mouse. He was always scampering off when I was on the range, but every morning he'd be back in my pouch sure as the sun rose."

"But how will I feed him?"

"He is a *field* mouse, Heloise. A ranger like me. He will feed himself."

The mouse stood up on his hind legs and faced Heloise, tiny nose sniffing the air, little black eyes fixing on her. His gaze was so intent and earnest that Heloise couldn't help but laugh.

"What shall we name him?" Clodio asked. "He is your mouse now, so you should do the honors."

Heloise looked at the little trembling body, considered. "I will call him Twitch."

Clodio nodded. "A good name for a good mouse."

"You're sure I can have him?"

"I am. A ranger's life can be hard even on a mouse. He would be much happier with a warm hearth and a little girl who truly loves him."

"There's no hearth in the vault."

"You won't be in the vault forever."

She reached out tentatively, and Twitch strained to reach her, stretching up on his tiny legs, short tail poked out for balance. "Does he bite?"

"Yes," Clodio said, "but not you. Never you."

Twitch jumped onto her hand. His claws raised gooseflesh as he scampered up her arm to her shoulder and down the side of her dress, vanishing inside the pocket at the front of her skirt.

She reached into it to ensure he was there, stroked the soft fur between the ears with her finger. His whiskers tickled as he turned to sniff at her, but Clodio was as good as his word, and he didn't bite her.

Heloise knew that Twitch couldn't really watch over her, but she had to admit, with the mouse in her pocket, she did feel safer. "Thank you."

"He'll look after you now. The Emperor knows he'll do a better job of it than I ever could."

She hugged Clodio again, careful to keep her pocket well away. "I'm so glad you're back, Clodio."

"As am I, my dear," Clodio said, his voice thick. "Now, run along, or Barnard will be wise to our little meeting, and I'll never hear the end of it. I'll check in on you in a fortnight or so. All will be well, Heloise. You'll see."

Heloise didn't want him to go, but the feel of Twitch's soft fur under her thumb helped give her courage. She gave him a final hug, not speaking for fear that she would cry again, and then she began her slow circuit of the house as Clodio's shape dwindled in the darkness behind her.

The stars wheeled overhead and the trees resumed their whispering and she was alone again. No, not alone.

"You'll watch over me, won't you?" she found herself whispering to the mouse in her skirt pocket, even though it made her feel silly.

9

FOUND

Hell slithers like the snake and burns like the salamander.
Hell bites like the winter and the blade alike.
From this font the wizard drinks,
And as the wolf pup shall gnaw on the innards of the
  dead,
Surely it so gnaws upon the soul of the man,
Until he is consumed, and the portal open within him.
            —Writ. Imp. III. 1

Heloise said nothing of Clodio's visit, or of his gift. Keeping secrets made for troubled sleep. She woke in the night, went fumbling her way over to the sack of candles. Her one hand felt Twitch, still nestled in her pocket. The other brushed the old stub of her candle and found it cold. She felt around for the sparkstone and the metal striker, set to sparking them together.

She froze mid-strike, listening.

Shouting, loud enough to be heard through the thick bronze. Men's voices, raised in anger. They came louder and more frequent, though the metal door prevented her from making out the actual words. She recognized Barnard's voice, his sons, a woman's, probably Chunsia's. Other men, one of whom sounded familiar.

Barnard's voice coming closer, still yelling. She could make out some of his words now. "Of course not! . . . Solid metal, it is! . . . impossible!" Heloise backed away from the door, waiting to hear the iron key rattling in the lock, the tumblers turning.

Instead she heard a knock. Then another. And another.

Three knocks. Danger.

"See? Solid metal," Barnard said.

The familiar man's voice said something she couldn't hear.

"I will not," Barnard shouted. "Only the Procurer may look inside."

More shouting.

Heloise looked frantically around, seeing nothing in the inky black. Was there anywhere to hide? She searched her memory of the space when it had been lit. Her heart pounded, her breath coming so fast it was hard to think. The racks on the walls were shallow, the unfinished works lining them not big enough to hide behind. The corners were bare. The only things in the tight space were the war-machines.

Heloise bent, scooping up her blankets, pot, food, and candles and climbing into one of the war-machines. She tucked her supplies behind her, and threw the blanket over one of the rods in the frame, letting it drape in front of her body before shoving her arms into the metal sleeves, just as the iron key rattled in the lock and the door swung open, Barnard still yelling behind it.

"The Procurer will hear of this, Holy Brother," Barnard was saying. "It will not go unpunished."

"You are a villager," the familiar voice was clear now. It was Brother Tone. Heloise could see the outline of his head and shoulders through the weave of the blanket. There were more with him. "You do not deal in punishment, but I do. And the punishment I will mete out on that factor will make hell itself seem gentle."

Barnard looked inside, and Heloise peeked out from beneath a corner of the blanket just enough to see the shock on his face. He had surely thought they were all doomed. "Well, as you can see, there's naught in here save the Imperial commissions, which are supposed to be a secret from all, even you, Holy Brother."

The light from the workshop came in behind Tone, so that she could see the grim set of his mouth, but not the zealous blazing of his blue eyes. "I decide what is secret and what is not here, villager." Tone looked up at the machine, and Heloise felt as if he could see through the blanket. She stayed frozen, not daring to move, not daring to breathe.

Tone looked around, eyes sweeping the racks and floor, his face satisfied until he looked up at the racks in the center.

"What are these? Armor?" Tone asked.

"War-engines," Barnard answered, "and more than you should see."

"I may see whatever I like when I am about the Emperor's business," Tone snapped. "Those blades look sharp on both ends."

"They are, Holy Brother," Barnard answered. "The shorter end is the tang."

"Tang? So they attach to this . . . war-engine?"

"To the fists, lord. Aye."

"Extraordinary," Tone said. "What is the blanket covering?"

Me, thought Heloise, her lungs beginning to burn from holding her breath. Had Tone already found her father? Her mother? Her eyes were dry from staring, tears starting to form at the corners, but Heloise didn't blink. *No movement. Not a breath. He must not see you.*

Barnard stuttered for a half moment as he saw the blanket and likely guessed what lay behind it. "The tinker-engine, lord. You've seen them before, they contain the seethestone that drives all such works. They must be kept dry, and even drafts carry water. A blanket suffices in here. If I were to move it, I'd use salted cloth."

Over Tone's shoulder, the workshop doors were flung wide. She saw a tiny white shape dart past them, tow-colored hair flying back from its shoulders. *Basina.* Heloise had to stifle the urge to cry out to her. Her best friend raced through the workshop doors and vanished into the night. Where was she going? To warn Sigir? The sentries would have sounded the alarm if the Order approached. He should already be warned.

Tone shifted his flail to his shoulder and stroked his chin. "Still. It must be enormous. Let me have a look." He stepped into the darkness of the vault and Heloise had to stifle a scream.

"Holy Brother!" Barnard shouted, snatching Tone's arm. "I could lose my head for allowing anyone to set foot in here!"

"You will lose your head if you do not take your hands off me at once!" Tone shouted back, shaking his arm loose and reaching with his free hand for the blanket over Heloise.

Horses whinnied outside the workshop doors, and Heloise heard the pounding of hooves against stone and earth. Tone turned, his flail head bouncing on his shoulder. One of the other Pilgrims was already racing out the door. He looked outside, turned back to Brother Tone. "The horses are gone, Holy Brother!"

Tone turned back to Barnard. "Don't think that I don't know what's happening here, Tinker."

Barnard bowed. "Forgive me, Holy Brother. Might be my hitching post is rotten."

"As rotten as your traitorous heart. If those animals are not found, it will come out of your skin."

"I will send my sons to help you look for them, lord. They won't go far, horses go to where there's grazing, and the best is on the common green."

"You had better be right," Tone said. He gave a final, long look at the vault. "Those really are extraordinary machines, Tinker. You do good work."

"Thank you, Holy Brother." Barnard bowed again as Gunnar and Guntar raced out the workshop doors, lighting torches as they went.

Tone swept out after them, his gray cloak swirling around his feet as he disappeared around the workshop doors, Bolt and Blade barking fit to wake the dead, following behind. Barnard went to the threshold, hand on the heavy wood, looking out into the night, no doubt making sure Tone was gone.

At long last, he hung his head and sighed. Only then did Heloise take a gasping breath, her vision going gray as she suddenly realized how hungry for air she had been, how badly the blanket had itched her face, caused sweat to run down her back. Barnard winced at the sound of her gulping air, looked back out the door, then turned back to her.

"You're fortunate he didn't hear that," he said.

"Is he gone?" she asked, throwing off the blanket and clambering down from the machine.

"For now. I never thought he would make me open the vault. These damned Pilgrims are only pious when it suits their needs."

"I think Basina spooked their horses."

"She did, brave girl. He'd have found you for certain otherwise."

"What about Papa? Mama?"

"I will go and see, but I don't think he found them, either. Tone would have enjoyed that too much to keep it quiet."

"Please," Heloise gasped, feeling her stomach tighten again. She couldn't bear not knowing if her parents were alive. "You have to find out and tell me."

Barnard knelt and ran a trembling hand through her hair. "I promise I will, Heloise, but it won't help anyone if they come back and you're found. We have to close the vault door now."

And suddenly Heloise was frightened again, as if she had used all the courage in her on keeping still when Brother Tone came into the vault and reached for the blanket. She was so tired, so relieved now that the Pilgrims had gone and the warm light of the workshop was spilling all around her. She couldn't bear to give it up again so soon, not before Basina came back. But Barnard was right, and after all Basina had done for her, the least she could do was be brave. "All right," she began.

"She doesn't have to go back in," Sigir said. "Not for the moment, anyway." The Maior stood in the workshop doorway, Gunnar and Guntar to either side.

Heloise ran to him, hugging him around the waist. Sigir put his arm around her and held her close. "There, there," he murmured. "It's over now. It's all right."

"Did you bring Papa?" she asked, all thought of bravery gone. "Please let me see him."

"Maybe tomorrow, Heloise," Sigir said. "They've gone for now, but they might come back."

"The horses . . ." Barnard began.

"Were on the green, as you said, Father," Gunnar answered. "They mounted up and rode off as soon as they had them in hand."

"That was a brave, stupid thing you did, girl," Barnard said, as Basina appeared from behind Sigir, her skirts in her hand.

"I had to do it," she answered, head high. "He'd have found Heloise for sure."

"Tone's no fool," Barnard said, "he knows it was no rotten hitching post what led to them getting free. We can only hope he thinks it a child's prank and not some kind of subterfuge. We'll know when he returns."

"He may not return," Sigir said. "He seemed convinced that Samson had run and taken his family with him."

Barnard snorted.

"I did right, Papa," Basina said. "You'd have done the same."

Barnard sighed, shook his head. "Being a father means being frightened every damned day of your life." He turned to Sigir. "We are betrayed. Poch, or maybe Sald."

Sigir shook his head. "You don't know that."

"Why else would Tone have wanted to look in the vault? Why would he even think—"

"No," Sigir cut him off with a wave of his hand. "They spoke against Samson, but that is not the same as betraying him to his death. Tone is a beast, and a clever beast at that. He will not leave stones unturned in his search. If it hadn't been for your daughter, he might well have found one of the Factors. We don't know that it was a villager what told him to look here."

Barnard shook his head. "I don't like it."

"There is nothing to like in any of this," Sigir agreed.

"Thank you, Basina," Heloise said, reaching out an arm and gathering her best friend into a tight embrace.

Basina hugged her back. "You'd have done the same for me."

"And I will," Heloise said with a sudden heat. "I will never let anyone hurt you. If Tone comes back I'll . . ."

"If Brother Tone returns, you will hide and keep quiet," Sigir said. "That is the best way you can keep Basina safe, keep all of us safe."

"Boys," Barnard said to his sons, "go down to the sentry tower and make sure they're well down the road. I'll put Heloise back to bed. I know you don't want to go back in the vault, girl, but there's nothing for it."

She felt Sigir stroke her hair, saw the Maior exchange a glance with Barnard.

"They could come back," Barnard said, but there was no resolve in his voice.

"I know," Sigir said, looked down at Heloise, "but I cannot bear this. Putting a girl in a prison. I don't think they'll come back tonight, Barnard. I just . . . I cannot bear it."

"Nor I." Barnard's voice was thick. "I'll set the boys on watches. If the sentry fails to raise the alarm, they'll call out should the Order return."

"Will that be enough?" Sigir asked.

"Enough time to get her into the vault if she stays just outside the door. There's the hounds, too." Barnard jerked his thumb at Bolt and Blade, already lying across the entrance to the workshop, backs to them, eyes warily set on the darkness outside.

"You mean I don't have to sleep inside?" Heloise asked, a smile already straining her cheeks.

"Close to the door," Barnard said, "and you sleep with one eye open. If riders do come, we'll need to get you inside as fast as a thought."

"I'll stay with her," Basina said. "You know how lightly I sleep."

Heloise's heart leapt at the thought. At last the reality of her hiding from the Order matched her dream of it, alone with Basina at night, sharing secrets. She reached into her pocket and felt Twitch there, his little pink nose brushing her thumb.

Gunnar looked up, frowning. "Father, I'm not playing nursemaid to these two. You know how they get when they're—"

"You shut your mouth, hammerhead," Basina said. "I'm betrothed now, and never asked for your minding even when I was still a maid."

"You are still a maid," Barnard laughed, "and I'm not eager to think of you otherwise, but you two will bed down here tonight, and the lads will keep watch outside. I can't sleep with the lot of you howling after one another. I've hounds for that work."

The boys looked as if they would protest, but went silent at a look from Barnard. "Yes, Father."

"You want to be sentries. This is what sentries do. Gunnar, you'll take first watch at the well. Guntar will relieve you at a half-candle."

"Yes, Father."

"And keep an eye on Poch, and Sald, and . . . and everyone," Barnard said to Sigir.

"You leave the village to me," Sigir said, "as I leave tinkering to you."

Barnard met his gaze, but said nothing.

"All right," Sigir said. "I'd best return to Samson." He gave Heloise a brief hug before letting her go. "I'll send your father your love," he said. "As soon as the Order moves on, we'll have you together again. I promise."

"Thank you, Maior," Heloise said, and then the men left them and they were alone together, just her and Basina, and the scraped and cooling crucible casting a dull orange light over them both.

"You saved me," Heloise said, felt how wide her eyes must have looked, how awed. Her belly tightened as she realized that she actually felt shy of herself before Basina, terrified she would say something stupid and ruin everything. That was silly, of course. She and Basina had been friends since they could walk. She was the same girl.

She wasn't sure what to say, so instead Heloise said, "You saved me," again.

Basina smiled. She might have blushed, but it was impossible to tell in the crucible's red light.

10

TOO FAR, TOO FAST

*Mahesh pierced Him with his spear, and the weapon stuck
    fast.*
*With His left hand, the Emperor did smite Mahesh on his
    crown,*
So that his head was cleaved in twain,
*And with His right, He drew the veil shut, sealing hell
    away forever,*
And died with a glad heart.
                        —Writ. Ala. I. 5

Heloise and Basina lay awake talking for the rest of the night.

The hounds were dim lumps in the dull glow of the cooling
fires, curled protectively in front of the doors and the people inside.
Heloise and Basina lay wrapped in blankets under the workbench.
Basina giggled when Heloise showed her Twitch, and shrugged
when she told her the mouse was a gift from Clodio.

"Promise you won't tell anyone," Heloise said.

"Why would I tell anyone?" Basina asked. "Rangers come and
go as they please, mice are everywhere. There's nothing to tell."

Twitch scurried between them, nosing at Heloise's blanket,
climbing over her hand.

"Oh, he's so darling!" Basina said, reaching out a finger for him.

Twitch gave a high squeak and Heloise giggled, picking him up. "It's all right," she said. "Basina is family."

"Oh, stop, Heloise. He's a mouse. He doesn't understa—"

But Twitch was raising his body up, balancing with his tail as he had when Clodio had handed him to her. His tiny black eyes looked at Basina, nose twitching toward her. "See?" Heloise asked. "He just needs some coaxing."

Basina drew back, eyes widening. "It's like he understands you."

"Well, maybe he does. He's my mouse, after all. That's what Clodio said."

Basina laughed, and held out her hand. Heloise coaxed the mouse forward with her thumb. "It's all right, Twitch. This is my best friend, Basina. If you're watching over me, you're watching over her."

Twitch looked over his shoulder at Heloise, black eyes considering. She could almost believe he understood the words as he turned back. Both she and Basina waited, holding their breath, until Twitch finally crept forward and sat stiffly in Basina's palm, tiny pink nose hovering over her thumb.

"It tickles!" Basina giggled, and Heloise felt as close to her as anyone in her life. Of course she could share Twitch with Basina. Of course Basina would understand.

Basina set Twitch to roam on the floor between them, but the mouse curled up in the folds of the blanket. Heloise left him, screened by her back from any curiosity from Bolt and Blade.

Heloise propped her head on her arm, looking at her best friend. The gentle glow of the crucible softened Basina's lines, until she seemed to melt and shimmer like a setting sun. Heloise could have looked at her forever. She didn't want to move, to speak, for fear that it would break the moment. It seemed as if all the heat of the workshop had gathered in Heloise's belly and thighs, a wonderful melting feeling. Her head felt like it was about to float off her shoulders.

Basina shifted, rolled onto her side, big eyes sleepy. "What are you thinking about?"

"You," Heloise said. "How you saved me."

"All I did was untie the horses and say 'boo' at them a couple of times."

"It's more than that. You're special. Like a hero from the Writ. I've never heard of a woman doing something like that."

Basina laughed, making her so beautiful that Heloise thought her heart would break. "I'm not a woman yet, but I will be soon."

"You mean your husband." Heloise felt a spike of cold through the delicious heat in her belly.

Basina nodded, and the cold spike sank deeper, driving the heat from her utterly. Heloise grieved its loss even as she tried to smile for her friend.

"They say it hurts," Basina said. "At least, it does for girls who don't run or ride. I rode a horse once, and mother says because I run a lot that—"

"Your mother talks to you about it?" Heloise asked.

"Who else? She's borne three children. She knows what she's about."

"My mama would never . . . she only said that when the time comes, I'm to lie back and be as quiet as I can."

"That doesn't sound nice at all." Basina frowned.

"It's not supposed to be nice."

Basina grit her teeth. "It is. Mother says that when you love someone, it's the most wonderful thing in the world, even if it does hurt at the start."

"And you love him?" Heloise tried to keep her voice from shaking, failed.

Basina didn't notice. "He's strong, and he's kind. He always calls me 'my lady' as if I were a princess! I like the way he looks at me. I think he would get good children. That's love, I suppose."

Heloise didn't think love was something you should suppose. She was sure she loved Basina. Sure in her bones and in her belly. She was sure that Basina was the most beautiful, the most wonderful person in the world, and that she would never love anyone else. More sure than she had ever been about anything in her entire life. That's what love should be, sure as stone, as running water. Sure as the bite of winter and spring blossoms. Sure even when it was impossible. Even when they were both girls.

"And . . . and you'll be happy, being married?"

"Why wouldn't I? You know it'll be you soon. Aren't you just a little excited about it?"

Heloise thought about it. She knew she was supposed to be looking forward to her wedding day, to an honorable future as a wife and mother. But the thought of her mother, crouching under her wimple before the hearth, the same four walls about her day after day, made her sad and sick in equal measure. "I don't know," Heloise said slowly. "Sometimes I think maybe I don't want to keep a home . . ."

"Why not?"

"I don't know . . . I like going with Papa on his rounds. I like going to Lyse on market days. I liked meeting the Kipti. I wouldn't want to stop doing that."

"With the right husband, you won't have to. Randal says I'll be able to rule the roost."

"Yes," Heloise said, "but he still has to *let* you rule it."

Basina shrugged. "That's the Writ. The Emperor's will, not ours. Anyway, I think you're just being contrary. I bet you'll love every bit of it, even the rutting."

Heloise laughed at that, swatted at her. "Stop!"

Basina smiled and they were silent for a while. Finally, Basina spoke.

"I've never done anything, you know . . ." Basina's voice was small, shy. She sounded very much like Heloise felt, a tiny thing in a bigger world that had plans for her whether she liked it or not.

"You never?"

"No!" Basina sounded annoyed. "I would never. I mean, once I would have, but Gunnar came along and ran him off. I was angry, but later I was glad. He didn't tell Father. Mother said that when you're young, your body can . . . betray you."

Heloise was silent at that.

"You never . . . ?" Basina asked.

"Me?" Heloise could feel herself blushing. "Ah . . . No. Well, once one of the Bricker boys tricked me into going behind the shrine with him, and he tried to kiss me."

"Did you?"

"No. Maybe a little."

"You were scared? Was he ugly?"

"At first I didn't mind . . . but then I worried that Papa might find out, and I kept thinking of Mother's face if she heard I'd been disgraced. Then I didn't like it and I ran away."

"My mother says it's not a disgrace so long as you don't do it with everyone and so long as it's just kissing."

Heloise laughed. Being near Basina in this perfect soft light made her feel like she was floating. "My mother would turn purple at that kind of talk."

"Well, I never have, and I'm . . . I'm worried about it."

"About kissing?"

"What if he doesn't like the way I do it? What if it makes him not love me?"

"Oh, Basina, no one could ever not love you." Heloise heard

the heat in her words, didn't care. She loved Basina. She loved her so much.

"You're kind to me. Still, I worry. I've asked Mother, but she only says that I'll know what to do when the time comes. But . . . what if I don't?"

The heat was back, boiling up inside Heloise and banishing the cold until she felt grateful that she was not standing, for fear her legs would betray her. "We could . . . we could practice."

Basina looked at her, eyes wide. "What, the two of us?"

Heloise's mind screamed at her to look away, to say Basina had misunderstood, anything but face the possibility that Basina would be disgusted at the thought. *No. You will be brave. You faced a Sojourner.*

"We could," Heloise said. "I mean, I'll do it, if you will."

Basina stared, and Heloise found herself blabbering to fill the silence. "You said you're worried about not knowing how to do it, and I was only thinking that if we tried it here, then you'd know what to do, at least a little bit more than you do now, and that way you . . ."

"All right," Basina said, sitting up.

"What?"

"All right. Let's try it."

The warmth in Heloise's belly flared, crept lower. It was a strange, new feeling. Her head spun and her vision swam. She felt dizzy, but for some reason she liked it. It was a moment before she could speak. "All right." *Oh, Sacred Throne. Oh, Emperor. I'm going to kiss her. I'm going to kiss her.*

"You can't tell anyone," Basina said. "If we do this. Just one kiss, just to practice."

"Oh, of course," Heloise could hear her words coming quick, tumbling over one another. "I wouldn't want anyone to know either."

They were both sitting up now, heads leaning close together. Heloise could smell the sweetness of Basina's breath, feel it against her neck. Her best friend's face was hidden in darkness, the edges lit by the soft glow of the crucible. "How do we start?" Basina asked.

"I . . . um. One of us should be the boy."

Basina nodded. "That's a good idea. Would you mind doing that? I need to practice being the girl. Not because of anything with you . . . it's just that you're not betrothed yet, so I'm the one who's going to need to do it for real sooner."

"Of course," Heloise said. "That only makes sense."

Heloise froze, terrified to move for fear that it would make Basina change her mind.

"So, you're the boy," Basina said. "That means you have to start."

"Oh, yes. Sorry. All right." But Heloise couldn't move, her body betraying her as Basina's mother had said it would, only in the opposite way she'd expected. The moment dragged out and Heloise feared it would be lost. She would be brave, like Basina was.

She pushed herself into motion, leaning into Basina, walking her hands forward on the packed earth floor.

Basina's breath came closer. Heloise felt her hair brush her forehead, the tips of their noses gently touching. Their knees bumped together. She felt Basina's cheek touch her own, realized that her friend was leaning in as well. Was there a part of Basina that wanted more than practice?

The thought sent ripples up Heloise's belly and out into the rest of her, making her skin tingle and her toes go numb.

And then her body truly betrayed her.

When Heloise was very little, her father had made a small boat for her out of dried leaves and tallow, and set it floating in a brook. The toy boat had been tossed and spun, ripped this way and that by the competing currents, until the fragile structure could take no more, and came apart in a shower of brown flakes.

Heloise felt like that now, the current of her love carrying her helplessly along. Her movements came as if from a great distance, her conscious mind only aware of the wonderful heat that ran from the bottom of her ribs to the tops of her thighs.

Her stomach was full of fluttering wings, her head stuffed with clouds. Her eyes closed and she saw stars bursting, like the fireflowers the Kipti had set off in the market square three winters past. She couldn't breathe, couldn't think, and didn't mind at all. *Oh, Basina, you are the most perfect person in the world. Oh, Emperor. Oh oh oh oh.*

Her hand reached out, grasping the back of Basina's neck, pulling her in. Every fiber of her body reached for Basina, and she found herself pressed solidly against the girl, amazed by how their shapes fit together. She wanted to be closer, couldn't get close enough.

Heloise felt as if she were drowning, but she didn't care. She didn't ever want to breathe again if it meant breaking away. She straightened enough to lift her other hand from the ground, pulling Basina with her, holding her close. Basina drew back, gulped air.

"Love you," Heloise heard herself murmur, tightened her grip on the back of Basina's neck, leaning after her, lips reaching for another kiss.

Finding nothing.

Basina gripped Heloise's wrist, strained to break her hold.

She was pulling away.

Horror curdled in Heloise's gut, the slow dawning of the realization that she'd made a terrible mistake. Too slow. For another moment, she refused to let Basina go. The crazy thought rose through her mind: if she could just kiss Basina again, it would be so wonderful that her friend's resistance would cease and it would plunge them both back into the bliss she'd drowned in just a moment ago.

But Heloise was a factor's daughter, her hands weak from years behind stylus and tablet, quill and parchment. Basina was possessed of the iron strength forged in her father's workshop. Heloise's hand broke away from Basina's neck. Basina reached out and pushed once, violently. Heloise flew backward, skidding on her shoulders, the rough blanket saving her from tearing her clothes on the packed earth.

For a moment, the two girls were frozen: Heloise propped on one elbow. Basina on her knees, face a pale mask of shock.

Say something. Fix this. The words raced through Heloise's mind, so many and so fast that they jumbled together, drowning in grief. An instant ago, she had been in the midst of the greatest joy she'd ever known, living a dream she hadn't known she'd been dreaming. And just as quickly, she was sinking in horror. Had she said she loved her? Basina didn't look like she loved her back. She looked terrified. As if Heloise had suddenly transformed into a giant spider, or a snarling dog.

"You . . . you . . ." Basina stammered.

The words were tangled in Heloise's mind, so her mouth finally moved on its own. Heloise forced a smile, barked a hysterical laugh. Somewhere in her panicked mind, instinct had decided that she could pretend it was a joke, all a terrible misunderstanding. Basina couldn't have really thought she was serious, could she?

"I was just pretending to be the boy. That's what boys do." Heloise heard her voice, heard the high, forced laughter, sounding like a madwoman. But she couldn't stop.

Basina's expression didn't change.

"Basina, I was only . . ." Heloise got to her feet.

Basina lurched back onto her haunches, put her hands out in front of her. "Don't."

And then the laughter tipped over. The hysteria remained, but the mirth slipped into sobs, and there was no more pretense that it was a joke. Heloise had done what she had done, and she couldn't take it back. And now Basina hated her, and the only refuge she had was gone. Why was she so stupid? What did she think would happen? She deserved whatever was coming.

Yet the tears would not stop, and Heloise stood, crying, while Basina overcame some of her surprise and said, "You said you loved me. Not like friends. Like a girl loves a boy."

Heloise could only nod, crying harder. *I do,* she thought, *and I've been a fool and I'm sorry, and if you'll only forget this and we can go back to the way things were, I promise I'll never do anything like it again. Please don't be angry. Please don't hate me. Please don't be frightened of me.*

But Basina no longer looked frightened. Her expression had gone hard. "Heloise . . ."

But Heloise had already turned, started running. Maybe there was a chance she could still fix things if she would only stay and try to reason with Basina. It was after dark, she was alone. The Order was out there. She couldn't go now.

"Heloise!" Basina shouted. "Heloise, wait!"

But Heloise's body wasn't done betraying her. She ran, tripping over Bolt and Blade, who yelped and snarled at her as she went down on her hands, scraping them raw.

She rose, went on running, digging in her pocket, desperate for the touch of the mouse's soft, warm body. She only felt cold cloth, coarse and empty beneath her questing fingers. She remembered that the mouse had been sleeping on Basina's blanket. He had likely scurried off when Basina had pushed her away. She was alone.

She scrambled to her feet as if a devil pursued her, and ran out of the door faster than she'd ever run. The tree line outside the Tinkers' workshop was a black cloud settled across the gray landscape, dusted with diamonds from the stars that shone overhead.

The devil on Heloise's heel was the realization of what she had done and the loss it assured. She ran with all she had to keep ahead of it. Branch tips stretched out to lick at her face as she cleared the first of the great trunks and disappeared into the depths of the wood.

Basina was betrothed. Basina did not love her. Heloise had lied to her, offered to practice kissing to help her be ready for her wedding night. But Heloise was gratifying her own lusts, not helping her friend at all. How could Basina call her a friend now? Now that she had betrayed her?

She forged deeper and deeper until all was darkness: gray, black, and the lashing thorns that were the kiss she knew she deserved.

II

FUMBLING IN THE DARK

I'm glad of Clodio. He's mad as a hare, but there's fight in him to his roots. After the fighting, he's always got us laughing, even old Sigir, who's as dour as iron.

Told us a story (not true, I'll be bound) of the time he was in the South, and met the Sodan of the Algalifes. A prince of princes there, Clodio said, yet he always wore an iron manacle.

Clodio said he asked the Sodan why, and the great man said, "For all my might, I am a mere slave to the Kali."

Not so different from us, then, these Algalifes. Even heretics have masters.

—from the journal of Samson Factor

Heloise lost track of how long and how far she'd run. The forest was a tangle of rough branches reaching out from the darker shapes of moss-covered trunks. The ground was a treacherous enemy. She couldn't count how many times she'd fallen, risen, gone on again. She only knew that she had to keep running, that if she stopped, she'd be forced to face what she'd just done. So long as she kept her mind busy with navigating through the rocks, roots, and branches, she wouldn't have the time to think about it.

The forest grew thicker, shutting out the moon and stars, and the darkness closed in around her like a physical thing, the smoke of a close and greasy fire. She inhaled it, the air as heavy as in the Tinkers' workshop, but cold now, and vile, stinking of the world taking back the dead into itself: rotting tree trunks and the carpet of dead leaves beneath her feet going slowly to mud.

Her body now launched its next betrayal. Her lungs began to burn, her breath coming in whooping gasps. Her legs went weak and refused to go on. She tried to drive them forward a few more steps, succeeded only in sinking to her knees.

And then the reckoning was upon her.

Her mind viciously recalled all that had happened. The warmth shooting through her body, the delicious drowning sensation, the giddy sense of floating on air. Basina pulling away. Her eyes going hard, her hands coming up.

The storm of memory broke and the tears came, overwhelming her. She pitched forward onto her hands. She gulped air, shrieked out her sorrow, heedless of whether the Order could hear, howling and stretching and finally forming into words. "I'm sorry!"

She heaved, collapsed on her side. Her eyes finally adjusted enough to make out the tree trunks nearest to her. They were giant things, larger than a man could circle with his arms. The moss clung to one in great clumps, giving the bark the appearance of a stern old man.

"I'm sorry," she sobbed again, but the old man's face in the tree had no forgiveness for her. The wind sighed in the branches and the ground was wet and cold against her side. It didn't care about her. Even Twitch was gone.

She could not bear the shame. She would close her eyes and will the breath out of her body. She was too weak to move anyway, and only pain awaited her any place she were to move to.

Her mother and father both had warned her about wandering off into the woods on her own. The traveling Kipti could come and steal her away. There could be brigands, or bears, or worse. The Order was somewhere out there, probably gathered about their campfires, raising their heads at the sound of her shouted apology. It didn't matter. Whoever came for her could have her. She stared at the old man in the tree's mossy beard. The green thickness seemed to ripple.

Rustling leaves told her that whatever danger her parents had predicted had found her. At first, she thought it might be the wind, but then she heard the pause and intake of breath as whoever it was spotted her, followed by the deliberate sound of footsteps.

She was frightened, but the fear washed into a pool of relief that it would soon be over. She closed her eyes. "I'm sorry," she whispered again, one last time.

"I know you are, child," a voice answered, soft and gentle, "but there's nothing for you to be sorry for."

Hard hands slid under her knees and neck, cradling her head gently, folding her into a chest covered in rough wool that smelled like old leather and leaf mold. She felt the top of a hatchet head bump against her.

"It's all right," the voice said again, sighing like the wind, and she recognized it at last. She turned into the narrow chest and sobbed anew.

"It's all right," Clodio said. "I've got you.

"I've got you."

· · ·

The ranger carried her in his arms like a baby. He hummed as he walked, a nonsense tune of deep murmurs that only just sounded like words. She imagined herself in the arms of the old man in the tree, only now his face was kind and his moss beard soft and sweet smelling, pillowing her head as his hard wooden arms cradled her gently.

It was a silly, childish thought, but it fit the sound of Clodio's humming, and for a moment the horror of what she'd done was kept at bay, unable to break through the bubble of safety Clodio had woven about her. He said he had her. He said she had nothing to be sorry for. It was the last shred of a life worth living, and she clung to it.

The ground finally gave up its treachery and went over to a steady, gradual rise, the trees thinning around them until the starlight pushed through the treetops.

One tree stood out above the rest, hugely thick around the base, rising straight until its trunk ended in a jagged, uneven line in the air, twice as high as a tall man. As they drew closer, Heloise made out a light flickering from inside and realized it was the stone ruin of the roundhouse. Clodio had left a fire burning when he came for her. Out here in the wild with the Order about, that was a bold move.

"How did you find me?" she asked.

The humming stopped. "So, you've your wits about you, eh?" he said. "Down you go, then."

He stopped and gently set her on her feet. She briefly clung to his neck, not wanting to leave the safety of his arms, but life couldn't be avoided forever. Here, with Clodio, she felt like she could face it.

She tested her legs, found they would hold. Clodio stood back from her, setting his knuckles on his hips. "You don't look too banged up, I suppose, for a girl running for her life through the wild wood on her own."

"You aren't answering me," she said. "How did you find me?"

He laughed louder than she thought was wise when anything could be lurking in the dark. "I had help from a certain mouse."

He held out his palm. Twitch stood on his hind legs, nose straining toward Heloise. He let out a small squeak at the sight of her.

She took him in her hand, bent her cheek to his soft fur. "I lost him."

"He came running, whispered in my ear, told me you were in trouble. Of course, he wasn't entirely sure where you'd gone, but he does have a better sense of smell than I. Got me close enough to hear you when you decided that you had something to say to the entire wood."

"Stop it. You're making up stories."

Clodio's face went serious. "Wizardry. Twitch is my eyes and ears, Heloise. I told you he would watch over you. I meant it."

Heloise's stomach turned over. "That's not funny."

Clodio shook his head, chuckling. "You're not to be denied, are you? Ah, I should know better than to underestimate you, Heloise. I'm sorry. Let's get some food in you and figure out what to do next."

Heloise heard a branch breaking out in the woods and looked over her shoulder. "But the Order—"

"Is camped on the other side of the village, and down the road besides," Clodio said. "They'll not trouble us tonight. Come and eat."

He started walking toward a darker patch in the gray surface of the ruined tower that Heloise assumed was a long-neglected door.

The talk of wizardry had rattled her. She was so happy to have Twitch back in her pocket, to feel his soft fur against her thumb, but she couldn't explain how Clodio had come by him. The woods were vast and dark, and Twitch was so very small. "I'm not hungry."

Clodio stopped, but didn't look back. "Well, sit by the fire then.

The night woods is no place for an unarmed girl to go a-walking, and as you say, the Order's about."

"You're certain they're not coming?"

"I'm certain. We rangers have ways of not being found when we don't want to be, even with little girls in tow."

"The Tinkers will be worried."

"They will. Even now they're readying to search for you, I'm sure. Daybreak is close at hand. Catch your breath and I'll take you back."

Heloise knew he was right, knew she had to return, but the thought of facing Basina after what had just happened made her stomach churn and her shoulders shake. "Please, let me stay here."

"Heloise," Clodio said, "the Tinkers will go mad with worry. How would you like them to turn an ankle hunting for you out in the dark?"

"That's not what I want," Heloise said, but the terror of facing Basina again consumed her, and she felt herself close to tears again. "I'm just . . . I'm not ready."

Clodio paused, sighed. "All right. You can stay until you've caught your breath, and then we have to take you back."

He started toward the roundhouse again and suddenly the darkness seemed very close around her, alive with crunching twigs and the wind breathing between the trees. She found herself hurrying after him. "I can't go back. Not ever."

"Really now," he said. "You killed someone, I take it?"

"No, of course not," she said.

"Ah, so you stole then. The Maior's gold candlesticks? His favorite horse?"

"What's wrong with you? You know I wouldn't steal."

"I do," he said as they reached the tower entrance, "but you're saying that you can't go back, even though the Order is out here, and you were crying about being sorry, so I keep thinking that whatever it is that has you running through the woods at night must be a terrible thing indeed."

But Heloise could hear his smile, and part of her thought he knew exactly what she'd done already. That he didn't seem angry, or disappointed, helped her master her grief.

"It is terrible," she said softly as they passed through the ivy-covered, rotten timbers that held up the tower stone and framed what had once been a grand door.

A filthy leather bedroll was laid out in one corner of the ruin, at the base of a stone staircase that wound upward for two flights before ending in midair, a jumble of blocks below showing where it had collapsed who knew how many years ago. The tower stretched above it, until it ended in a jagged and roofless circle open to the sky.

A small fire was built in the ruins of the staircase, burning merrily under a little iron pot. The ruin was empty, overgrown and dirty, and felt as safe as a fortress. Heloise looked up at Clodio to find him gazing down at her, dark eyes reflecting the dancing flames, the ever-present smile lifting the corner of his mouth.

"It is terrible," she said again.

He nodded. "I believe you. It's just that I'm having a hard time picturing what it is that the Heloise I know could have done that was so bad. You've killed no one, stolen nothing. Ah!" He snapped his fingers. "You desecrated the shrine of the Emperor! You pulled the statue down and pissed on it."

She gasped in horror at the blasphemy, though her heart delighted in the plain talk. "No! That's disgusting!"

"But you said you'd done something terrible. No murder, no theft, no blasphemy. You're too young for a ravishing . . . So . . ."

He went to her side as the tears doubled her over again, walked her to a block of broken stone smoothed with time, and sat her there. "Heloise, you ravished no one. I know this."

"I . . . I . . ." she managed between hiccupping sobs, struggling to speak. Her fists were balled in her lap, and she could feel Twitch as he nosed out of her pocket and licked at her knuckle.

Clodio knelt before her, his dark eyes finding hers, holding them. She tried to look away, found she could not, her tears drying as she lifted her head.

"Heloise," he said, kneeling before her, hands on her knees. "Heloise, listen to me. Will you listen?"

The words were a question, but they sounded like a command. She nodded.

Clodio rocked onto his backside, folding his legs in front of him, resting his elbows on his knees. The firelight danced along his face, shadowing his eyes and making him look very tired.

"Your father will have told you about my payment for the heart-fruit rind." He sighed.

She nodded, and he sighed again.

"What did he tell you?" Again, Heloise felt as if he already knew the answer, and was asking the question for her rather than him.

"Mother," Heloise said. "She said that you loved too much. So much that it hurt you. She said it was as if your heart were too big."

He smiled sadly. "She's right. I did love too hotly, and it has hurt me, and my heart has brought me grief.

"But this is the thing, Heloise, and you must remember it. If nothing else in our friendship stays with you, I ask that you only remember this one thing, can you do that?"

Heloise nodded, leaning forward. "What?"

"That love is worth it. It is worth any hardship, it is worth illness. It is worth injury. It is worth isolation. It is even worth death. For life without love is only a shadow of life." He gestured at the fire beneath the pot, his hand fading to gray in the wavering shadows. "It is like my hand now. Looking the same, but drained of all color. It is a living death."

"What did you love?" She asked.

"Not what, silly girl. Who. Only other people are worthy of the kind of love I am talking about. Oh, the Order will tell you that you should love the Emperor more than anyone else, but it's a bunch of claptrap and they know it."

"Who was it? What was she like?" she asked.

He looked up at her now, his face a mask of sadness. For a moment she could see the young man Clodio had been, the hopeful man ready to risk anything. She could imagine his own traitor body, dragging him on.

He shook his head. "No. It is a person you love. Not a name. Not a she or a he. A person in all their shining glory. There is a thing in us, Heloise. A seed. It makes us who we are. It is our core. That is the thing that we love. It alone exists. It alone is holy. It has no home, no name. It is neither male nor female. It is greater than that. Do you understand?"

He knows. The thought sent chills through her. *And perhaps . . . perhaps it was the same for him.*

"I loved a *person*, Heloise. I loved this person with all of myself. It was a thing I have never known before and will never know again, and I would have done anything for it."

"What happened? She . . . the person didn't love you back?"

"The person did"—his voice was suddenly so low she had to strain to hear it—"but love is a great power. As with wizardry, such a power cannot be permitted to flourish outside the Emperor's grip. There are those who wish to possess love utterly, to own it not just for themselves, but for all. Do you know how they possess it, Heloise?"

She didn't even nod this time, staring at him openmouthed and silent.

"They own it by defining it," Clodio said. "They say 'love is this' and 'love is that' and when others say it is something else, they imprison them, or flog them. Sometimes they kill them. My love was a thing outside the circle they had drawn. It made them angry. A mob of them gathered, and they chased us. We escaped, only barely, and after that the person I loved grew afraid and sent me away and will not answer me any longer."

A tear fell from one eye, sparkling in the firelight before vanishing into his beard.

"Then it wasn't love." The words bubbled up, as the grief had, escaping from her mouth before she could control them.

Clodio looked up at her, eyes angry, but the words seemed to have a life of their own, refusing to be bitten back. "If a person loves as you say, then they would never send you away, no matter what the world would do to them," she said.

"Then what are you doing running through the woods, child?" Clodio asked.

Heloise bit her lip and looked at her lap. Twitch disappeared back into her pocket.

Clodio rocked back to his haunches and gripped her knees again, seeking her eyes. "I'm sorry, that was cruel. Please forgive me. Here is what I meant to say. Never be sorry for loving, Heloise. No matter who it is, no matter how it is done, no matter how the person you love receives it. Love is the greatest thing a person can do. Most go their entire lives knowing only ritual and obligation, mistaking it for love. But you have loved truly, as few can ever hope to do, and so young. This pain you are feeling is a triumph, Heloise. It is a crown as great as the Emperor's own. It means you can love, and that means you are good. Loving is never wrong, and nothing that comes from loving can ever be wrong. Never forget that."

She slid forward into his arms, wrapping her own around his neck, sobbing afresh. "Sh— . . . she looked at me . . . like she wanted to hit me." *Wait*, Basina had said, but it had only been because she knew the Order was outside, because she had been sworn to protect her.

"I know," Clodio said. "It doesn't matter."

"How can you know?"

Clodio's eyes crinkled as he smiled. "Twitch told me everything."

"Stop it! What if she never speaks to me again?"

"Then you will hurt, and you will change, and you will be someone else, but the good in you will live, Heloise. No pain in the world can kill that."

And he held her as she wept for what felt like hours. At last, she had shed all the tears she had, and lay exhausted against his shoulder, gazing into the dying firelight, feeling his hand stroking her hair.

She slid away from him. "Thank you."

"You are most welcome. So, now you see. Now you see what it is like to have people condemn you for who you are."

She nodded.

"And what do you think of that, Heloise? How do you feel about people punishing you for having the audacity to love?"

"It's . . ." She felt the embers in her, the pain and grief giving over to something else. Anger. Why should she have to hide her love for Basina? So that she could be a good, obedient Imperial subject? So she could have the pleasure of someday holding a wooden pole while a village burned?

The ember was small, but it grew quickly, and it felt so much better than sorrow.

"The Order, Heloise," Clodio said. "They are at the root of it all. The Writ tells us how to speak, how to eat, how to work, how to love. It withholds everything from us. Knowledge, freedom, power."

He leaned forward with each word, the firelight dancing across his eyes. Heloise felt the hairs on the back of her neck stand up. "You weren't joking. About how you knew. About Twitch."

He shook his head. "I am a wizard, Heloise. Without wizardry, I would have died in these woods half a dozen times at least."

She scrambled to her feet, heart hammering in her chest. She reached for Twitch again, but the touch of his fur did nothing to calm her. The shadows were suddenly close around them, pressing in, hungry. "You reach into hell . . ."

"Hell is a word men use in place of fear," Clodio said. "No one knows what lies beyond the veil, not even I, who touch it every chance I get."

"The portal! You'll become a . . ."

He reached for her and Heloise turned to run, but he only set his hands gently on her shoulders, looked into her eyes. "Heloise, listen to yourself. You believe the lies they've fed you since you were a baby. What is more evil? Wizardry? Or the laws against it that stands a little girl in a Knitting cordon, making her bear witness to slaughter and pillage?"

Heloise shook her head. His words made sense, but her insides crawled at the thought of the taint leaking through his fingertips and into her soul. "Heloise, look at my eyes. Tell me what you see."

Heloise bit back tears of terror. "No. You'll . . . you'll . . ."

"I'll what? Do you even know what wizardry does?"

Heloise tried to think, to remember the stories, the warnings of the Writ, but the truth was she knew only hints. Wizardry would make a man strong, or it would make his teeth long and sharp like a wolf's, or he could spit fire.

"Heloise, please," Clodio said. "I'm your friend."

And then she did look, though the panic nearly choked her, gooseflesh standing up on the backs of her arms.

Clodio's eyes were deep and dark and smiling.

"What do you see?" he asked.

Her own reflection stared back at her, her nose looking too big and her eyes too small. "Nothing."

"No portal? No devils reaching through?"

"No," she said, the fear slowly giving way to a heat in her cheeks. Stupid girl.

"The Order tells stories to frighten you. Wizardry isn't evil, Heloise. There is no blight. It is simply a thing that makes men strong, maybe stronger than them, and like love, they seek to have mastery over it. For without that mastery, they might be opposed, and lose their place over us."

"What does it do, then?" Heloise asked.

Clodio's face crinkled into a smile. "Let me show you."

He stood, put his fists on his hips, looked around the circle. His brow furrowed in concentration. He looked confused, old. Doubt pricked at the back of her mind. He snapped his fingers, his face lighting. "I've just the thing. Let's give you a more comfortable place to sit." He stretched a hand over a patch of bare ground beside the fire, grit his teeth.

Nothing.

Heloise grieved then. Because if Clodio was crazy, then all his talk of love and goodness had been mad ravings. Like Churic. The sort of talk that got villages condemned. False. Dangerous. The warmth that Heloise had felt, the safety, drained out of her in an instant, the grief and terror rushing back in.

In her pocket, Twitch grew suddenly still, his little nose pulling back from her fingers.

Clodio blinked.

The patch of ground beneath his hand vanished. In its place was a sudden movement, a mass of quivering black, shuddering and swaying and growing tall.

Grass. In spite of the early autumn frost, it was sprouting madly. In moments it stood as high as her waist, a divan, like noblewomen lay upon, as long as she was tall. It pushed its way up through the packed ground, green strands twining together like serpents, braiding themselves, then lying down neatly, until they had formed a pallet that looked thick and soft. Lamb's ear sprouted at the head, the broad, fuzzy leaves overlapping one another until they made a deep pillow that fluttered slightly in the warm draft from the fire.

Heloise couldn't help herself, she clapped her hands together in front of her chest, feeling a smile stretch her cheeks.

Clodio laughed, bowed. "Your seat awaits, Imperial Majesty."

All her life, Heloise had been taught that wizardry was the greatest of evils, hell's window into the world. She had imagined even its benefits to be dark and terrible, men grown to the size of giants with fire burning in their eyes.

She looked back at the divan Clodio had made for her. It was incredible in its way, but in the end, it was a simple and familiar thing.

Clodio gestured to his eye. "No portal, Heloise. I have used wizardry every day of my life for ten winters now. Wizardry is not devils and death. It is not flying or breathing under water. It is beds and food and water to drink. It is warmth in the winter. It is healing. It is life."

Heloise wanted to believe him, but couldn't silence the voice screaming at her to flee.

"Try it," Clodio gestured to the divan.

Heloise knelt, reached out a hand, pulled it back. Clodio rolled his eyes, squatted beside her. "Heloise, it's me. I've known your father since you were a babe-in-arms. Have I ever lied to you? Have I ever turned a false face to your family? Just touch it."

And Heloise did reach out then, holding Clodio's eyes the whole time, looking for a trace of a lie, for a glimmer of a portal's edge. She saw only the man she'd known all her life, the same laughing wrinkles that had always made her feel so understood.

The divan felt soft, the grass giving gently at her touch and then springing back. Her body cried out its exhaustion, reminding her of how much the last few hours had taken out of her.

Clodio saw it. Nodded. "It's safe, Heloise. Sit."

Heloise sat, felt the springy cushion of the divan take her weight. There was no blight, no scent of hell. She only felt the comfort against her legs, the intense desire to lie down. She was so tired.

But the fatigue struggled against her curiosity. "This is what wizardry does? Makes chairs?"

Clodio laughed again, and the sound chased her fear away. "Wizardry does many things. Some of it depends on the wizard. The rest depends on where they are and who taught them."

"Who taught you?"

"No one"—he shook his head—"which is why I'm not very good at it. I imagine a real wizard wouldn't be very impressed with what I just showed you. I have focused on what I know, the world around me. Wizardry has taught me the language of the plants and rocks and the animals that live among them. People, too, though I have to push hard to reach them. Wizardry is, in the end, another way to talk to living things. A more convincing way."

"You . . . convince plants to grow?"

Clodio nodded. "This is why I range, Heloise. The land gives me everything that your village gives to you. What it can't, I trade for. I keep my own counsel, away from the judgments of the Order and those that do their bidding."

"Like the Kipti. Mother says they're wizards."

Clodio laughed again. "Stories. I have met three Kipti in all my travels. None of them spoke to me of wizardry. None of them showed any sign of it. People are far more . . . complicated than animals. To convince them is a mighty work indeed, and I've found it's easier simply to be careful about choosing one's company. For the most part, I choose none at all."

Heloise had always thought Clodio's life hard, taking her cues from her parents' pitying glances and warnings to take care with him. Looking around the ruin, she saw it differently. The fire burned merrily, the grass pallet soft and warm beneath her. Clodio had all the comforts of village life, with none of the limits. He could come and go as he pleased, work as he pleased, love whom he pleased.

"But the Order . . . they'll . . ." she said.

Clodio's smiling face went hard. "Wizards are not so easy to kill, Heloise. Brigands tried to take me in the wood outside Porter's Rock three winters ago. They failed."

"You killed them?"

"I spoke to the wolves. What they did with the brigands, I did not stay to see."

"Can you teach me?" The words came tumbling out of her mouth before she could stop them, and her stomach turned over at the blasphemy.

Clodio's face stayed serious. "Not everyone has a talent for wizardry, but I can try. That is a conversation for another day, when you are less tired. It's time I took you home."

"I'm not tired," she said, though her eyelids felt heavy. "Is Twitch really wizarded, then? Did he really speak to you?"

Clodio smiled. "It's nearly daybreak, Heloise. If I promise to tell you, can we go?"

Heloise nodded.

Clodio grit his teeth again, not moving. Long moments dragged. Heloise drew breath to ask him what he was doing, when Twitch suddenly burst from her pocket, jumping to the ground.

"Madam," Clodio said, "I present your protector and guardian, my eyes and ears. Master Twitch, the wizard mouse."

Twitch twirled on his hind legs and, with a high squeak, made a sweeping bow.

Heloise squealed with delight, clapping her hands again. "Oh, Clodio. That is so wonderful!"

Clodio nodded. "He's a nervous one, our Twitch, and hard for me to understand at times, but he loves you as dearly as I do, and he will never fail to look to your defense."

The mouse stood stock straight, holding an imaginary spear over its tiny shoulder, and marched back and forth.

"So, that really was how you knew what happened? Twitch told you?"

"Yes. This was why I never feared for your safety. While Twitch is with you, so am I."

"What else can he do?" Heloise asked. "Can he speak to me, too?"

"Now, now." Clodio waggled a finger at her. "I have fulfilled my part of the bargain, so you must honor yours. It's time to go back."

"I'm not ready," she said, but there were no tears this time. "Can't I stay here with you? You can teach me to talk to him."

"We've stayed long enough," Clodio said. "Any longer and we'll make even more trouble for the Tinkers. When next we meet we

will see if you still want to learn how to talk to animals yourself.
I promise."

Heloise nodded, though the terror made her legs feel weak.

She would go back, she would face whatever consequences her
actions with Basina would bring. But it seemed a small thing now,
silly and distant. Because she knew she didn't have to wait to
know if she wanted Clodio to teach her wizardry.

She already knew she did.

12

VENGEANCE

*The servant to his lord, and all the people unto the
    Order, the Hand of the Emperor,
Working His will. As the rope keeps the raft from breaking
    apart on rough water,
These chains held the people fast together, and they
    knew peace.*
                        —Writ. Heb. L. 46

Clodio saw her as far as the woods' edge. "It was risky enough for me to come see you when the sun was down," he said. "Best not to risk it now."

"I know the way from here," Heloise said, her voice trembling. The protective bubble Clodio spun had been broken the moment they stepped out of his camp, but here was the place where she must step outside even its hollowed remains, and she found that she was not ready.

Clodio smiled, showing yellow teeth. He put a narrow hand on her shoulder. "The Tinkers will have questions, but you don't need to give them answers. Not until you're ready."

She nodded, sniffling in spite of herself.

"There, girl," Clodio said, "all is well. Do not forget what I told you. Love is good, and those who love are good. You have done nothing wrong."

"And you promise you'll teach me?" She searched his face, hoping for some hint of the smile she'd seen in the night.

"I promise we will discuss it. You're sure you can go on your own from here?"

She smiled, still sad, still frightened, but strengthened by the mouse in her pocket. "I think so."

"Good. I'll be back as soon as I can. I've a commission in the north that will have me away for a fortnight, but I'm hopeful to find cobalt there, and then I can return and fleece your father for all he's worth. By then, the Order should have moved on and this will all be done with."

Heloise laughed and Clodio laughed with her, some of the exhaustion dropping away from him. "You're a good girl, Heloise," he said. "I only hope someday this wicked world can come to deserve you."

And with that he had turned and was walking back into the woods, his long legs carrying him into the maze of trunks until the shadows swallowed him.

·   ·   ·

Heloise walked to the line of shadows that marked the forest's edge. Beyond the wave's edge of gloom, the overgrown grass grew in long tufts, thick with dandelion despite the lateness of the season. The last of the moonlight washed over it, so bright it shone.

Her house reared up in the distance. She could see no one about, heard no sound but the wind sighing in the trees.

She tried to take a step forward, could not bring herself to do it.

Heloise wasn't sure when she'd put her hand into her pocket, but she felt Twitch's tiny pink tongue licking at her finger, his sharp teeth gently grazing the surface. She gave him a scratch.

He felt so warm, an ember in her hand. The heat gave her strength.

"I'm not alone," she said. "You're with me, aren't you, Twitch?"

As if in answer, the mouse rolled himself into a ball that filled her palm.

"Forward together," she said, and stepped into the light.

The heat vanished. Twitch scampered to the opposite side of the wide pocket, and all the sound that had been missing suddenly came rushing into this new, moonlit world.

The sight of her house nearly brought her to tears again. A fire had burned nearly constantly in the hearth for as long as Heloise had lived, and in its absence birds had already begun nesting in the chimney, digging out tufts of the thatch. Squirrels chased one another over the flagstones that led to the door. It was shocking how quickly the world had moved to reclaim her home. It looked as if she'd been away two years, not two days.

She shook her head. It didn't matter. It was just a pile of wood, wattle, daub, and thatch. If her father and mother weren't there, she didn't want to be either. The thought made her heartsick for her father. She looked up at the silver of the moon, starting to give way to the dawn. Surely if she went to Sigir's first, the Maior would let her see her papa? Just for a moment. Just long enough to embrace him and feel that he was alive. Then she would face the Tinkers. She needed to see her father. For strength.

She lifted her skirts and hurried on, angling away from her house, away from the Tinkers' workshop, toward the Maior's house instead. She couldn't bear to face any of the Tinkers now, least of all Basina. The very thought made her stomach clench.

She ran faster to chase the thought from her mind, focusing her eyes on Sigir's tinned gables, growing closer through the trees. It was still so early that there was no one about to see her, and she ran faster still, hope blossoming in her breast. Maybe Sigir would let her stay with her father for just one night. He could go and tell the Tinkers that she was well and safe, and that they need not search for her, and maybe it would be best for all if she just stayed in his cellar with her father and . . .

The sentry horn sounded, low and long. It was Harald Brewer's voice that carried faintly on the wind, calling out the warning. "'Ware riders! Cloaks and flails! Cloaks and flails!"

Heloise stopped so quickly that her heels dug up the ground, nearly sending her tumbling. She glanced back in the direction of the Tinkers' workshop. She had run far from it, and the way back led her past the sentry tower and directly into the path of the riders. It was a shorter run to Sigir's house by far. Sick terror churned in her belly, making her arms and legs feel leaden, slow.

Heloise ran into the trees, angling straight for Sigir's front door. The branches pressed against her, as if they wanted to hold her back, deliver her up to the Order. She pushed through them, bursting out of the wood and racing the rest of the way to the split rail fence along the flagstone path to Sigir's door.

The horn sounded again. "Throne be praised! The Emperor's Own are come to us!" Harald called. He would only be shouting that if the Order could hear him. That meant the riders were entering the village now. They must have been coming at a gallop.

Heloise let her momentum carry her into the thick goldenwood door of the Maior's home, striking it with her shoulder hard enough to rattle her teeth and make the brass fittings tremble. She pounded her fist on the door, fighting the urge to cry out, careful not to make a noise that might alert the coming riders to the presence of a girl of sixteen winters here. "Papa, Papa, please. Open the door!" She whispered to herself. "Please!"

She stepped back, waited. Nothing. No one was coming. She knocked again, as loudly as she dared. Silence.

The horn again. Harald didn't call this time, which meant he had sounded the horn and immediately gone to the ladder, was coming down from the tower. The riders were in the village.

She could wait no longer. They would likely ride straight here, address the Maior as was customary. She had to be gone by then. Heloise turned and ran for the Tinkers' workshop.

She could feel Twitch bouncing in her pocket, put a hand inside to steady him. Her breath was coming harder now. She was whispering in spite of herself, couldn't stop. Over and over. "Sacred Throne, protect me. Emperor, hear my prayer."

Hoofbeats. The Pilgrims. She was gasping so loudly that it was hard to tell if they were coming closer or moving farther away. Best to keep running. The track to the workshop rolled out before her. She could make it.

Shouts. The hoofbeats sounding louder. A jingle of spurs, of iron chain.

There was a loud stomp and suddenly a wall of black rose up before her. Heloise dug in her heels, still ran into it, her forehead banging against something soft and warm and firm. She reeled back, the smell of leather and horsehair filling her nose.

"Heloise Factor." Heloise followed the voice up the back of a tall, black horse. The same blazing eyes, the same tucked chin. The faintest hint of a yellowed splotch, a bruise nearly healed. Brother Tone grinned fiercely. "The Emperor's will is always done. Sooner or later."

Stupidstupidstupidstupid. She cursed herself over and over. She had to try to see her father. If only she had done as she was supposed to and gone back to the Tinkers straight away.

Heloise turned to run, saw more horses all around her, their legs a shifting forest she could not hope to escape. Gray cloaks swirled on their riders' backs. The flails were down now, heads dangling from their iron chains just above the earth. If there had been ten Pilgrims in the village when Tone had threatened

Basina, there were ten times that number now. It looked to Heloise as if every Pilgrim she'd seen on the road to Hammersdown
was here.

A slash of red emerged from the whirling gray. The Sojourner,
his flail alone still hanging over his shoulder. Eyes widening as
he recognized her. "The Throne's providence," he whispered.

"Indeed, Holy Father," Tone agreed. "If the child is here, the
father can't be far. That Tinker was hiding something, I know.
The Maior, too, I will put them both to the question. They will
tell us where they are."

"You have much to learn." The Sojourner smiled. "There is no
need to question anyone. Make the girl scream loud enough, and
the parents will come."

Tone looked up at the Sojourner, frowning. "Holy Father?"

"What does the Writ tell us, Brother Tone?" the Sojourner
asked. "The Emperor is more pleased by one hare snared than the
scent of two."

"Yes, Holy Father." Tone jerked his flail into the air, sending
the head swinging toward her. The sudden motion made Heloise's guts turn to water, and she did scream, a tight shriek of "No!"
loud and piercing. *Oh, please, Papa. Don't hear me. Please don't
come.*

It was Sigir's voice that shouted answer. "Heloise!" the Maior
called, racing toward her from the sentry tower. He must have
stood the watch himself that night, wasn't home to hear her when
she banged on his door. "Heloise!"

Behind him came most of the village men, Sald and Poch,
Harald and Danad, others. Many of the women, too. She could
see Chunsia and Basina, but not Barnard and the Tinker boys.
Perhaps they were still out looking for her. There were more villagers than had frightened the Pilgrims before the Knitting. But
this time, the Order numbered as many as the villagers, all in

their saddles, flails at the ready. They circled warily, keeping Heloise boxed in, more than enough of them to watch her and the gathering crowd at the same time.

Sigir reached them and tried to push through regardless. "Heloise!" he called to her. "It's all right, girl!"

Tone wheeled his horse, pushing Sigir back with one iron-shod boot. "You lied to me." He sounded genuinely hurt. "You lied to the Emperor's Own."

"I am Maior here!" Sigir shouted, as if that made a difference now.

"It's as if you lied to the Emperor Himself," Tone said. "You said she had run with her father. Where is he?"

"Heloise!" Another voice, choked with tears, winded with running. Even through the panting she recognized it. Her father, her father running to save her.

"Get away from her, you damned cowards!" Samson shouted. His hair was wild and his clothes filthy, and even from here Heloise could smell the stink of shit on him. *The privy. That's why he didn't answer the door. He was hiding in the privy.*

"Give me my daughter!" Samson shook his fist, light flashing from a long, broad-bladed knife. He swung it as he came, reaching for Tone. But her father was a pikeman, trained to the long spear. The blade was clumsy in his hands, and Tone touched his spurs to his horse to move out of his way, tapping him on the back with his flail butt as he went. Samson stumbled to his knees, wrapping his arms around Heloise. She buried her face in his neck, ignoring the stink, feeling the throb of his pulse and knowing that he was alive. "Papa," she whispered. "You came."

Samson squeezed her tightly before leaning back, running his fingers over his face. "You're all right? They didn't hurt you?"

She nodded so quickly her chin touched her chest. "They didn't hurt me, Papa."

"Oh, Samson." Sigir sighed. "You great fool. You've killed us all."

Brother Tone reined his horse around again, closing the circle of Pilgrims up. "Samson Factor," he said. "The Emperor provides."

Samson stood, tucking Heloise behind him. He held the knife out in front of him. It looked tiny and useless surrounded by the forest of ready flails.

Tone smiled. "I thought I was going to have to put at least one person to the question to find where you'd gone. And here you are in the common. I can't believe you didn't flee this place when you had the chance."

Tone moved his horse toward them, reined back at a thrust from Samson. "Come on, you bastards," her father whispered. "Come on."

Brother Tone leaned forward in his saddle and pointed at her father. "I *told* you I'd come back for you. Did you think me a liar?"

"Enough," the Sojourner said. "Kill him and let's be done."

Brother Tone stiffened. "The Maior too, your eminence. He lied to us. This is his village, and it is for him to ensure his people keep to the Emperor's Writ."

"Here I am. You cowardly bastard." Sigir pushed against one of the Pilgrim's horses, trying to force his way into the circle. "Come down off that mare and leave your flail. We'll see who the Emperor favors."

Tone laughed. "You'd like that, wouldn't you? To brawl with one of the Emperor's Own, drag us down into the mud with you. The Emperor chooses who He will, and births us into the stations that fit our souls. Mine is to bring His word to you benighted savages, to ensure you don't open the gates of hell and condemn us all. Yours is to lord over those who scratch in the dirt and make sure you keep us in food, clothing, and implements of war."

"Enough!" the Sojourner shouted at Tone. "The Maior too.

Have it done." He turned his horse away. "I ride on. Attend me when you are through."

Her father and the Maior. After all this, they meant to spare her. They would kill her father and Sigir and leave her alone.

Before she knew what she was doing, Heloise bent, picked up a rock, and threw it. Her aim was good, honed by years of skipping stones off the pond. The rock sailed through air suddenly gone thick, seeming to move slowly, all eyes turning to follow its path. It smacked into the side of the Sojourner's head, knocking his hood askew. His horse shied and he yanked on the reins, angrily pulling the animal around, fumbling at the scarlet cloth suddenly drawn across his face.

"Coward!" Heloise shouted. "You tell your man to kill people and then you can't even bear to stand around and watch it."

The Sojourner finally yanked his cowl back into place and glared at Heloise. "Idiot girl! What do you think you're doing?"

She knew what she was doing was foolish, that she would only make matters worse, but it didn't matter. She was in thrall to the rage now, the anger as sudden and hot as an oven given a blast from the bellows. "I was in your stupid Knitting, and there was no wizardry. You lied because you wanted to kill and steal. You're not holy men. You're just a bunch of brigands."

"You will shut your mouth." The Sojourner's face had gone as scarlet as his cloak.

Heloise was dimly aware of the danger, of the gathering frost in the Sojourner's eyes, flecks of black gravel that darted left and right, taking in the Pilgrims, all watching their master challenged by a little girl.

"You will learn your place!" the Sojourner snarled.

But Heloise couldn't stand aside. Even if the burning rage would allow it, she realized now that something had broken inside her when she'd stood beside her father and watched Hammersdown burn. It might have healed in time, but the look in Basina's eyes had ensured the fragments were so small and so scattered that they could never be pulled together.

She raised her fists, took a step toward the Sojourner's horse and the animal shied a second time. "My place is between you and my father."

The Sojourner's head followed his eyes now, jerking side to side, desperately searching the faces of his Pilgrims, the villagers around him. "Someone deal with this child."

It was a command from deep in his throat, a mummer's voice, designed to preach to the far corners of the giant nave at Lyse.

But no one moved. The Pilgrims looked down at their saddles, at the ground below them, at the villagers, anywhere but at their master.

"So be it," the Sojourner said. "Here we see the red among the gray. I will do the deed myself."

"No," Sigir said, ducking under a horse's neck and dashing out in front of the Sojourner, "she's just a girl."

But the Sojourner's flail was coming off his shoulder, the butt thumping into Sigir's stomach, driving the Maior to his knees. Heloise watched the Sojourner dig in his spurs, the huge muscles of his horse's shoulders bunching as the animal plunged forward. She dimly heard her father shouting, leaping to save her, waving his knife, sharp and deadly and too short to be of any use at all. She could see Barnard and his sons now, coming at a run at the edge of the circle, too far away and not fast enough to do any good.

The moments stretched out as Heloise realized how tiny she was, how empty her hands were, how far the flail reached. She watched the black iron spikes on the head spin slowly into a blur. As time seemed to slow, her mind sped up, choosing and dismissing a dozen strategies. There was no way she could outrun a charging horse.

Heloise stood where she was and closed her eyes.

It would hurt, but only for a moment. And then it would be over, and she would never have to face Basina or her family, would never have to lie awake thinking about Hammersdown and what she could have done to save it.

She reached into the pocket of her skirt, hoping to stroke Twitch one last time.

The mouse was gone.

She heard the flail head jerk on its chain, could feel the air as the black iron spikes spun through, cutting their way to her head.

"Stop!"

When Heloise was little, there'd been a storm, so loud and so terrible that she swore it was happening right over her house. The thunder rang so powerfully that the air vibrated, making the wattle shake and her ears hurt.

The shouting voice was as loud as that thunder, and Heloise winced in spite of herself, opening her eyes. She watched the flail jerk up, the head bouncing on the end of its iron chain, spikes nearly close enough to brush her nose. The Sojourner had turned, staring opened-mouthed at the circle of villagers, parting to admit a single man.

Clodio.

The old ranger seemed to glow. His clothing was still ragged, his skin still as brown and cracked as old leather, but it was different now, like the look of well-worn tools, hardened from use, stronger than ever. Clodio seemed taller, his thin limbs longer, his eyes brighter. A tiny mouse sat on his shoulder, perched on its hind legs, little muzzle thrust into his ear. Twitch. Twitch gone from Heloise's pocket to get help.

"You will not harm her," Clodio breathed.

The Sojourner snarled into the silence. "Now, all see why we are here. A wizard among us, standing in our very midst!"

He stood in his stirrups, holding out his flail. He was pale, and Heloise could see the ruffling of his cloak where it masked his trembling leg, but his voice was steady enough. "You will kneel and submit to the Emperor's justice."

"No." Clodio smiled. "But you will submit to the winds beyond the veil. You will ride out, and you will harm no one, and should you come again, I will not be so kind."

The Sojourner dug his spurs in savagely, raising his flail. "Cleanse the filth!" he cried, and the Pilgrims took up the call, Samson and Sigir and all the villagers forgotten, their horses wheeling and plunging toward the lean old man, who stood with his arms outstretched, grinning like he was mad.

Clodio swept his arms up, and Heloise heard a rustling, a sound like the ripping of fabric, so loud that it made her ears ring. All around them, the earth exploded, clods of dirt and rocks flying into the air. Heloise saw tendrils of something flail upward, writhing like gray snakes. After a moment, she realized what she was seeing: roots. The thick taproots of trees breaking free of the ground and waving in the air.

The Pilgrims' charge halted as the horses screamed in terror and plunged in all directions, ignoring their masters' sawing on the reins, dragging the bits until their mouths bled. The Sojourner alone kept his horse straight on, swinging the flail about his head. "Fall before the Thro—" Something long and dark lashed out, slamming down on his horse's neck hard enough to send the animal crashing into the dirt. The Sojourner kicked free, tucking into a roll that snapped the broach at his breast and ripped the scarlet cloak from his shoulders. He came up on his knees, spurs flashing, the flail crosswise in his hands.

Heloise heard a creaking groan and ripped her eyes away from him.

Two of the giant oaks that ringed the common had detached themselves from the line of woods and advanced on the Pilgrims. One raised the long branch it had used to crush the Sojourner's horse, sending it sweeping into the Pilgrims' ranks, bowling them from their mounts like straw dolls, sending them flopping into the grass.

Tone dug his spurs into his horse's flanks and turned it sharply, charging to his master's defense. The second tree followed, slamming a branch into the earth so hard that Heloise felt it shake, showering them all with leaves and acorns. Tone's horse shrieked, rearing and plunging, lashing out with its hooves so hard that Tone abandoned all hope of control, concentrating only on keeping his seat.

The trees spun and lashed, spun and lashed, branches rising and falling like threshing flails, leafy crowns shaking above them. A few of the Pilgrims tried to fight, their iron flail heads digging furrows in the thick bark, but the trees showed no reaction. Their thick roots slithered up from the ground, yanking the Pilgrims down to the earth and crushing them there, until Heloise heard the crunching of bones and the men lay still beneath their gray cloaks.

The villagers scattered, streaming back as if the common had been set alight. Only Heloise and Samson remained, huddled together in the common's center, Samson desperately trying to shield them from the trees. He needn't have bothered. The trees whirled and struck, wreaking havoc among the Pilgrims, but they were careful not to come near the Factors, their branches only ever reaching toward them to snatch away a Pilgrim who tried to make for the Sojourner, who was even now rising to his feet, lifting his flail to strike.

Clodio, still grinning, dropped his arms and advanced to meet him. The Sojourner swung his flail over his head like an axe, and Heloise cried out, certain that Clodio would have his head crushed like Alna Shepherd's. But the ranger snatched his hatchet from his belt and swept it up, parrying the blow, twitching the head so that it tangled in the flail's chain, holding it fast. He leaned in close, grinning wider. The Sojourner grunted, eyes wide, desperately trying to pull the flail free, but Clodio might as well have been a tree himself for all the good it did him. The flail scarcely budged as Clodio slammed his head forward, the hard front of his skull smashing into the Sojourner's teeth, snapping the man's head back. Blood sprayed from the Sojourner's mouth and he staggered, eyes still wide, but glazed now, confused.

Clodio shook his head, teeth dropping from where they'd been lodged in his skin. He leaned in close to the Sojourner. "Where's your Emperor now?"

He twitched his wrist and the hatchet slid out of the flail's chain, spinning in his hand. He drew it up and yanked it forward, burying it almost to the haft in the Sojourner's chest. The Sojourner staggered backward, eyes still unfocused, sinking to his knees as a stain of darker red spread across the scarlet of his tunic.

Tone shouted, sawing his horse left and right. All around him, the remaining Pilgrims cried out, pointing at their fallen master. Clodio locked eyes with Tone, smiled. "Run along, now."

He put a boot on the back of his hatchet head, still buried in the Sojourner's chest, and shoved the man onto his back. The Sojourner sprawled in the grass and was still.

The Pilgrims turned and fled. The few who were still mounted slapped their horses into a gallop, but most just ran, clumsy in their heavy armor, flail heads bouncing over their shoulders. Tone cried out to them, cursing them for cowards, calling on them to stand in the Emperor's name. They ignored him, and at last he cursed and turned his horse, galloping to their head, leading them out of the village.

The trees followed, tottering on their slithering roots, trailing black earth behind them. They struck down two more Pilgrims before they stopped at the common's edge, suddenly going still. The common, too, was still, the shredded grass strewn with blood and freshly turned earth, littered with corpses wrapped in gray cloaks, flails snapped like matchwood, horses with broken legs, screaming out what life remained to them.

The villagers stopped their running and pressed back around the common's edge. Samson slowly straightened, his arms still wrapped around his daughter. No one spoke, all eyes were locked on Clodio.

Twitch finished his whispering and leapt from Clodio's shoulder, scampered in a straight line across the churned earth, light and fast as an arrow. Heloise felt his tiny claws scrabble up her leg, across her hip, and into her pocket.

Her hand chased him in of its own accord, and she stroked him with her little finger, feeling him soft and warm and trembling.

Clodio stood, swaying for a moment, eyes unfocused. At last he blinked and looked at Heloise. "Are you all right?"

"Oh, Clodio. Thank you."

"Are you all right?" he asked again.

"I'm fine," she said. "Are you?"

"That is the greatest wizardry I've ever worked." He waved, knees trembling. He swayed again, looked as if he might fall.

Heloise tried to run to him, but Samson's arm around her waist stopped her. "No!" her father hissed.

Heloise pulled against his arm, confused. Clodio had saved them. "Let me go!"

"He is a wizard!" Samson said, and Heloise realized with a start that her father didn't understand what wizardry really was. None of them did.

"It's all right, Papa," she said, pushing against Samson's shoulder, trying to break free, but his grip was like iron.

"It's all right," Clodio said, looking at Heloise. "I just need to rest. Twitch is back with you?"

Heloise stroked the tiny mouse in her pocket. "Yes, he's here. Oh, Clodio. I'm so sorry. Tell me you'll be all right."

"Fine." Clodio was already turning, lurching like a drunken man. His legs folded beneath him and he sat down hard. "Just going to rest. Stay with your parents. It's all right now."

Heloise flailed behind her, struggling to break free. She had wanted nothing more than to see her father again, and now with his arm around her, all she wanted was to break free. "Clodio!" she shouted.

Clodio slumped on his side, one of his legs kicked feebly. "S'alragh . . ." he rasped.

Heloise felt hot tears running down her cheeks. "We have to help him!"

"We have to stone him," Sald Grower shouted. "He's a wizard!"

"Shut it, Master Grower!" Heloise shouted, her cheeks suddenly hot. "He saved your life!"

"What do we know about such a sickness?" Sigir asked. He had walked up beside her family, the village coming behind him, gazing awestruck at the wreckage Clodio's wizardry had wrought. "How can we mend him?"

"We have to try," Heloise said. "Let me go, Papa. He's my friend."

"He's friend to us all," Barnard said. "Or . . . he was."

"He's a wizard," Samson whispered. "You have to beware the blight."

"There's no blight!" Heloise shouted, shaking free of her father at last. She spun on the villagers, her face red and heart pounding. Behind her, her friend was dying, and all they could do was stand there like frightened children. "I was in Clodio's camp last night. He made me a divan out of grass, and nothing bad happened! The Order tells everyone that wizardry is evil, but it isn't. He just used it to save your lives!"

"Evil may be used to a good end," Sigir said. "The Writ says . . ."

"It doesn't matter what the Writ says!" Heloise shouted, her cheeks burning, the anger blazing in her chest once again. Sigir flinched back from her, though he was a man grown and at least twice her size. "He's our friend and he helped us and now you have to help him! Where is Deuteria? Someone help me get him inside."

"Heloise," Sigir said. "He cannot stay here. He is a wizard. The Order . . ."

"The Order is beaten! Didn't you see? They are gone."

"They will come back."

"Then Clodio will be rested and he will beat them again, and this time we'll help him. We don't have to be frightened anymore. Don't you see? We don't have to Knit anyone. We have to help Clodio get better so he can help us again if the Order comes back."

"Heloise, that is heresy!" Samson shouted. "You will be quiet!"

"I will not be quiet!" Heloise shouted. "I'll help him myself if you won't!" She whirled, narrowly escaping her father's grasping fingers, raced to Clodio's side.

"She has a point, Samson," Barnard said. "Whether we turn Clodio out or no, the Order will be back for vengeance. Our best chance to stand against them is to make Clodio well."

"There is no standing against the Order," Sigir said. "We must flee."

"We just stood against them!" Heloise shouted as she knelt down over Clodio. "We stood and won!"

Samson shouted as she cradled Clodio's head in her hands. The ranger's jaw was slack, a thin strand of drool leaking from one corner. His eyes stared sightlessly past her shoulder. His chest heaved, breaths coming sharp and short.

Samson charged forward three steps and stopped short, terrified to touch Heloise now that she held the wizard's head in her hands. "Heloise! Come away from him at once!"

"Look around you!" Heloise shouted back. "Do you see any blight? Where is the rot and the horror? Where is the fire? He needs help!"

The villagers looked around them at the silent trees, roots still trailing dark earth. The wind sighed in their boughs, sending leaves skittering. Other than that, there was nothing. Everything went on as before.

Barnard grunted. "The girl is right. I will fetch Deuteria."

Sigir caught his arm. "It is bad enough that we were saved by a wizard. We can't give aid to one."

"That's not just a wizard." Barnard shook his arm loose. "That's *Clodio*. He stood in the pikewall with us, remember?"

The terror in Sigir's eyes turned to shame, and he looked at his feet, but he made no move to help.

Heloise slapped Clodio's cheeks, chafed his wrists. He did not respond. "Help me!" she shouted at her father. "He's dying and I don't know what to do!"

Samson turned to Barnard, and the big Tinker nodded. Samson cursed and the two of them jogged toward Heloise.

Leuba caught Samson's wrist. "No! I can't lose both of you!"

"What are you doing?" Sigir shouted. "I am Maior, and I say we flee!"

"To what end?" Barnard asked. "We will be a village of brigands. The Order will pursue us to the ends of the earth now. If we flee, we buy ourselves time. Nothing more."

"We will have to find a new way, all of us," Sigir pleaded. "The Kipti ply their trade from their wagons, never staying in one place for long. Perhaps in small groups, we can find other villages that will take us in. We can scatter."

"That is no life," Samson whispered.

"It is life," Sigir replied, "and now it is all we can hope for."

"Remember what you told me after you spoke for me in the gathering hall?" Samson asked.

"Aye," said Sigir, "but this is different."

"It's no different and you know it. In your worst moment, I'd have never cursed you for a coward, Sigir." Samson shook his head and knelt at his daughter's side. Barnard tried to join them but Samson waved him away. "You've no more skill here than I. Go fetch the herber."

Barnard grunted and jogged off. Sigir tried to stand before him, but the tinker brushed him easily aside. "Where are you going? I am Maior!"

"If you'd leave a comrade to die," Barnard didn't break stride, "then you're no Maior of mine."

Samson put his hands under Clodio's arms and lifted him. Heloise grabbed his boots, amazed at how heavy such a small man could be. Clodio's head lolled, his body as slack as if he had no bones, his skin gone gray as a corpse. Only his chest, rising and falling as fast as a rabbit's, gave any indication he was alive. "Where do we take him?" Heloise asked.

"The shrine," Samson said. "If the herber doesn't come, then the least we can do is pray."

Heloise's shoulders burned and her arms shook, but she held

on tight. She would not drop Clodio, not after what he had done for her in the woods, not after saving them all. She would hold on to him until her arms fell off. *You are not going to die.*

Leuba stood and took a few tentative steps, stopped, hand outstretched. The rest of the village clustered closer, but all stopped behind Sigir. "Don't be a fool, Samson!" Sald shouted after him. "Think of your girl!" called Harald.

Samson ignored them, grunting as he half-walked, half-fell backward toward the shrine's spire. The building was enormous by the standards of Lutet, its spire so high that it could be seen from atop the Giant's Shoulder up the Hammersdown road. It bore the golden eye of the Emperor's vigilance at its peak. A Sainted Palantine was painted above the double doors, hand extended, wings outstretched above his golden armor. A devil lay crushed beneath him, one of his armored feet on its neck.

Samson paused to get a better grip on Clodio, then hurried up the dirt path toward the doors. Clodio jerked, suddenly going stiff, his feet tearing out of Heloise's grasp. She stumbled back and Samson swore as the ranger's boots thudded against the earth. He tried to drag Clodio on his own, but the ranger was twitching now, his head thrashing from side to side, spit flying from the corners of his mouth, his teeth clenched so tightly that Heloise worried they might break.

Samson laid Clodio down as gently as he could.

"What do we do?" Heloise asked. Ingomer Clothier had been prone to fits when he was a boy. The only thing Heloise could remember was that you were supposed to make sure they were on something soft, so they couldn't hurt themselves by thrashing, and to put something in their mouth to keep them from breaking their teeth. But the cold ground beneath Clodio was nearly as hard as stone, and his teeth were so tightly clenched that she wouldn't be able to get a piece of parchment between them.

Samson had knelt, gripping Clodio's head between his knees, stopping him from knocking his skull on the ground. He tried to grab Clodio's flailing arms with his free hands, succeeded in grabbing one, only to have it ripped away when the other clouted him on the side of the head.

Heloise dove for Clodio's feet, stilled the drumming heels for a moment. But she was a girl of sixteen winters, and Clodio's legs were strong from years of ranging. His boots rose and fell, lifting Heloise with them, and each time she felt her grip shaken, the tips of the ranger's toes slamming painfully into her hips. At last, he kicked her free, and Heloise sprawled on her back.

"Help me, girl!" Samson shouted, Clodio's head still firmly gripped between his knees, reaching for his waving arms. "Get up!"

Heloise jumped to her feet, her hips and stomach singing with pain where Clodio had kicked her. She had been kicked by one of Poch's mules last winter, and had worn that bruise for the rest of the season. This felt almost as bad.

Clodio had pushed his wizardry too far to save them, and now he was going to die. She couldn't let that happen. She had to help him. Where was Deuteria? She cursed herself, cursed the whole damn village, standing by in their belief in the Order's lies. She thrust her hand in her pocket, drawing strength from the warm touch of Twitch's fur while she caught her breath.

A sharp, stabbing pain in her finger.

She yanked her hand out of her pocket, brought it up in front of her face. Two bright pinpricks of blood had appeared just below the half-moon of her fingernail. They blossomed as she watched, the crimson glowing in the dawn light before streaking down her hand.

Twitch had bitten her.

She sucked on her finger while she opened her pocket and looked inside.

Twitch was curled on his side. Heloise's heart leapt into her throat. Was he dead?

Then he thrashed his tiny head, spreading the bead of blood on his mouth out to soak into the fabric beneath him.

Her blood.

His body went stiff, little limbs sticking straight out, then slowly curling back in.

Does he bite?

Yes, but not you. Never you.

"Heloise!" Her father shouted. "In the Emperor's name, help me grab his arms!"

But Heloise stood staring at the mouse in her pocket. He rolled onto his back, little arms and legs kicking into the air, tail pin straight, the blood from her finger whipped to froth in his rapidly working jaws. A steady sound came from his mouth, low and creaking. Not squeaking, not the sound a mouse should make at all. She picked him up, lifted him out of her pocket, brought him closer to her face.

"Heloise!" her father called again, then Twitch shivered and split and changed.

She bit back a scream, forced herself not to drop the tiny mouse, or whatever he was now.

His tail was gone. His little nose still sniffed the air above the whiskerless snout. One eye was closed, the other opened so wide that it took up the entire side of his tiny head. The pupil was yellow, slit black down the middle like a cat's eye, wide and staring. His fur had come away in patches, leaving most of his side bare. Scales showed beneath, silver-green and shining, like a garden snake made of emerald.

Her pet mouse was gone. In its place was this mismatched thing. Slipped of whatever had held it together, it began to come apart in her hand.

It couldn't be. Wizardry was good. It had saved her. Twitch still felt like the piece of the world that stood between her and everything that loomed around her, her night with Basina, the Knitting, the Order.

Samson looked at her hand, gasped. He let go of Clodio, scrambled back on his heels.

It didn't matter, for Clodio had stopped twitching, was sitting up, shaking his head. He blinked, looked around, his eyes wide and confused.

The ranger's voice was as dry as a creek bed in summer. "Heloise? What are you dag . . . here?"

Heloise tried to speak, to ask him if he was all right, to ask how to help him, but the confused look in his eyes and the twitching creature in her palm made words impossible, and in the end, she only held up her arm, fingers spread to show the thing that used to be Twitch straining and kicking in her hand.

Clodio frowned, confused. He reached out, stopping short of touching the thing that had once been a mouse. "I don't understand," he said. "What's this?"

"It's Twitch," Heloise managed. "The wizardry . . . went bad somehow."

Hearing Clodio speak, knowing that he could think well enough to talk to her brought a spasm of relief, and she sobbed, a great hiccup of air that made her hand move.

Clodio kept looking at the spot where her hand had been, his eyes out of focus. His words slurred like a drunken man. "No . . . no, s'not raaaaght. S'not how it works."

He raised his head, eyes clearing as he found Heloise's face.

She dropped the thing that was Twitch and screamed.

Clodio frowned again, his eyes glazing over once more.

But all Heloise could see was his left eye, catching the thin light, white distorting into a cherry color sliding across the surface, a smooth, unbroken shine the color of the Sojourner's cloak.

Save one flaw.

A white line, glowing as if from within, rising straight, then curving at the top, like a tree bending in the wind.

Or the crack of a doorway, just beginning to open wide.

13

DEVIL

I lay me down upon my bed,
Thinking upon the words He said,
Given us in His Holy Writ,
To save us from hell's fetid pit.
I pray to live His holy word,
And be spared of His righteous sword,
And I shall never disobey,
Spare me, oh Sacred Throne, I pray!
—Children's bedtime song

"What?" Clodio asked, raising a hand, reaching for her. "What's wrong?"

"No!" Heloise shouted, falling back. "Don't touch me!"

"Heloise!" Samson cried, reaching for her. "What's wrong?"

Clodio turned to look at him, and Samson shouted, jumped to his feet. "Sahmshon," the ranger rasped, swung his face back to Heloise.

Over her shoulder, she could hear the villagers shouting now, Sigir calling to them to get back.

True to the Writ, hell was coming.

Clodio's eye throbbed, bulging until it was twice the size of the other. A thin trail of blood tracked its way from the corner down the side of his nose.

"Whasss gotten into you?" he asked. "I'm not gonna hurt you."

His right ear turned black, withered, dropped off his head, sticking to his shoulder before slowly sliding down his back and out of sight.

There was a crack of thunder, the sky above them abruptly darkening, storm clouds boiling over the tops of the trees suddenly, a gray curtain thrown over the common.

Heloise's heart hammered in her chest. Her breath came in whooping gasps as she took another step backward, her heel catching on a root. She sat down so hard her teeth clicked painfully, her mind screaming at her: *stupid stupid stupid.*

Clodio stood, bent toward her. "You're hurting yehrself." His voice sounded wet, as if he were speaking through a mouthful of curds. "Stop screaming."

She scrambled back on her palms before flipping onto her knees, scratching them painfully on the hard ground. Samson's ink-stained hand snatched her under the elbow, yanking her to her feet and propelling her toward the knot of villagers, side-stepping now, some of them beginning to run. Heloise saw the terror etched on their faces and felt it kindle her own.

She gave in to the fear and let it set her feet to running. She heard howling behind her, howling that sounded like talking, like a person calling out to her, desperate and lonely and in need of help. She hit the line of villagers at the edge of the common and burst through.

"Heloise!" It was an effort at speech by a mouth not made for words, a voice gargling through packed gravel. If it had been an animal, Heloise wouldn't have been frightened. She had lived beside these woods all her life. She knew hungry animals. This was something different, sounding just enough like Clodio to shake her to her bones. She glanced over her shoulder.

The thunder pealed again and fat drops of rain began to fall. Heloise felt them striking her face, her shoulders, cold and thick.

"Heloise," the thing that was Clodio croaked again. A crack appeared in its eye, working its way slowly down the center of its body. White light spilled forth, dazzling in its brightness. A sick stink came with it, powerful even from this distance. What was left of Clodio continued to move toward her, taking shambling steps, quaking arms outstretched as it split in half.

The grass beneath it shriveled and died, first shrinking, then graying, and finally reducing to a thick, black slime. It oozed outward, as if Clodio's step infected the ground, spreading to consume root and rock and Pilgrim's corpse alike, turning all the same fetid, liquid black.

Heloise stumbled, turned, tried to find her father, but he was lost in the press of villagers. They were backing away slowly, and she could hear pounding feet as the ones furthest back broke and ran. Where was Basina?

She heard a wet slurp and looked back up at Clodio.

No. Not Clodio. Not anymore. A new thing was pushing up and out of him, stepping through the shimmering, stinking light, rolling its shoulders and shaking off Clodio as if he were an old cloak. The ranger pooled on the ground, split and ragged, like a sheet that had blown off the drying line. The thing that unfolded from inside him reared up and shrieked.

She had thought such a giant would have a deep, throaty roar, but instead it cried high and piercing, like a hawk's call on sighting prey. The sound hurt her ears, sent chills through her.

It was nearly as tall as the shrine's spire, taller than any house in the village. Spade-shaped scales covered it, a mix of ill-looking colors, the purple of sick flesh, the yellow-white of rotten bone.

Six arms ended in clawed hands, each with five fingers ending in gray claws, dirty and hooked and sharp. Her eyes skipped over the thing, so stunned by its appearance that they kept leaping from detail to detail, unable to focus. A long black dewclaw sprouting below a knee the size of a tree stump. A pale body, not unlike a man's, the color of rotten fish. Rippling shoulder joints: two, four, six.

At last her eyes found its face and stopped.

It didn't match the stories. Heloise had always expected a man wreathed in fire, face contorted in rage around a mouth full of sharp teeth.

The teeth, at least, were sharp. They stuck out from a smaller mouth than she'd expected, sloping up as though it had been cut into the long face, a sculptor's mistake discovered too late to repair. The thing's two eyes didn't line up, one high on the forehead and the other in the space left by the rising mouth. The eyes squirmed, wriggling toward her. Each circle was a bunch of smaller white eyes, stalked and pale like poisonous mushrooms. There was no sign of a nose, only two black cuts in the center of the face. Long horns corkscrewed up from its head, arcing unevenly until they nearly met above it. The tiny mouth snapped once, twice. The eye bunches curved, narrowed. It screamed again, and the raptor cry made Heloise's ears ring.

A devil. Come through the portal in a wizard's eye. Just as the Order, the Writ had warned her since she was old enough to understand.

It charged, and the villagers all broke and ran, scattering in all directions. They needn't have worried. The devil arrowed straight for Heloise, reaching as it came.

It wanted her.

Terror blossomed in her gut, so fierce that it overwhelmed her, boiling in her head and nearly blotting out her sight. Her body belonged to the fear now, no more under her control than the devil itself. She forgot about Basina and her father and everything other than the need to run.

Heloise stretched her legs and ran like she had never run in all her days. Her legs burned and her throat felt as if she'd swallowed a bolt of cotton, but still she ran, listening to the thundering of the devil's steps behind her. The big creature was heavier, slower, but its strides were so much longer, and she could smell it as it drew nearer. It stank of rotting leaves, the slime of dried pools, of tree trunks gone to their graves on the forest floor. The odor was deep and earthy, so thick that Heloise gagged.

The storm was coming on in earnest now, the rain falling so hard that it lashed her face, soaking her through in moments. Her pounding feet kicked up puddles of wet mud. *Don't slip, don't slip,* she repeated to herself, over and over, praying that the muddy ground would slow the devil. Judging from its steady tread and the rising stink, it wasn't.

She ran like a wild animal, with no plan other than escape, but if her mind didn't know where to go, her body did, and she soon saw the rain-lashed slate roof of the Tinkers' workshop in the distance. Bolt and Blade circled before the great doors, barking with the savage enthusiasm that only dogs can muster.

Heloise sprinted through the opening, and the heat of the workshop enveloped her, blessedly warm after the run through the chilling rain. Barnard stood inside the vault door, the iron key in his hand, mouth open in shock.

"Devil!" Heloise shouted. "Run!"

"Heloise!" Barnard gestured to the vault. "Get in here!"

But the terror would not let her go back into that vault. Heloise pelted past him, heading deeper into the house, but Barnard reached out and seized her wrist. His grip was as strong as an iron vise, and Heloise nearly flew off her feet before she arrested her momentum, stopped. She tried to tell him to run, that the devil was behind her, that this was all her fault, but her lungs were on fire and she couldn't breathe and in the end all she did was put her hands on her knees and cough.

Bolt and Blade were yelping and running into the workshop. A boom shook the ground outside the doors and Heloise saw the devil's massive, scaled foot slam down, spattering mud so far that drops landed on the crucible's edge and disappeared in sizzling puffs of smoke.

"Hide, girl," Barnard said. He yanked on her arm, swinging her across him. Heloise went, staggering, helpless against the tinker's strength, not understanding his aim until she felt the cold air of the vault touch her, went sailing through the door.

"No!" She shouted. She couldn't be shut up in here. Not now. Not when all this was her fault.

She threw herself against the door, trying to wrench it open. "No!" she managed. This was her fault. Her fight. She had to be in it.

But the tinker's strength and the door's weight were far too much for her, and the last thing Heloise saw was Barnard snatching up his long forging hammer as the door slammed shut.

She tensed for the hungry darkness to seize her. There was no sack of candles for her this time, no way out if Barnard fell. But she blinked as the light remained, dancing orange and yellow, sending shadows spooling against the walls. Barnard had lit candles, three at least, and set them to burn on the vault shelves.

That wasn't all he'd done.

One of the war-machines had been taken down off its rack. It stood on its metal feet, back rigid, helmet held high. Heloise could smell the acrid tang of seethestone. Barnard had attached a giant shield to one of its metal arms. It was featureless, so long that it covered the machine from face to knees. It looked heavier than the workshop itself, and Heloise didn't doubt that its weight would crush a man without the tinker-engine to drive it.

A warhammer lay on its side in the dust, its metal tang pointed at the slot on the war-machine's empty fist. Heloise whirled away from the machine and back to the door, hammering against it. She could hear the dogs barking, Barnard calling to his sons, their short replies. Metal scraping and boots pounding. And then, the devil's eagle scream, high and piercing.

Boom.

The vault shook, dust raining from the rafters above her. The tinker-engines jumped on their shelves, rattling toward the edges. A small length of pipe rolled off one of them and clouted Heloise on the head before clattering against the war-machine's leg and falling to the floor. She leaned to avoid a canister that followed, looked around for shelter. There was nothing, the shelves too narrow to offer any real protection should the roof come down.

Boom. The devil was hammering on the roof. She heard wood splintering above, and a single slate tile shattered at her feet. Heloise darted across the floor and scrambled up the war-machine's leg, wriggling onto the padded ledge in the center. It had hidden her from Tone, it would have to shelter her from the devil now.

The inside of the war-machine was close and dark, and Heloise could feel the weight of the thick metal all around her. It made her feel trapped and safe at the same time. Barnard had buckled the straps, making leather loops inside the machine's hands, elbows, chest, and feet. Heloise wriggled into the chest loop, still kneeling on the padded ledge that would be a seat for a man grown. If she stepped off, her feet would dangle in the air, too far from the foot loops to reach them.

Boom. Another crack from above her. Something thick and heavy slammed into the war-machine's head, hard enough to rock the machine to the side. It tottered, and for a moment, Heloise worried it would fall over, but the shield acted as a counterweight, and it righted. She saw the fragment of a thick beam on the floor. Three more slate tiles fell beside it, bursting. Stone shards pattered against the war-machine's metal legs.

Heloise put her arm into the metal sleeve of the machine's left arm. She was able to hook her elbow through the leather loop in the elbow and reach the one in the war-machine's hand, but that left her right arm only just able to grab the elbow strap in the machine's right arm. Her eyes were still level with the metal gorget. She cursed her age. If she were just a little bigger, she could drive it. If only she knew how. It seemed simple enough, but she couldn't be sure unless she started the engine. The salted cheesecloth bag of seethestone hung beside her head, the chute leading to the engine canister beside it. Beside the chute was a metal handle that would pull the canister lid shut, trapping the gas inside and powering the machine.

Even if she loaded the canister, she would need water to set the stone to seething.

Boom. The vault shook. Cracks appeared above the bronze door, spidering upward. There was another splintering crash, more beams and tiles banged off the machine's top. If only she could drive the machine, she could knock the door down, get out of here. *And then what? Would you go out and fight the devil?* But Heloise knew she would. Here, encased in the dark weight of the war-machine, she wasn't afraid anymore, only frustrated, furious at her height and the length of her limbs, at her ignorance. *Sacred Throne, please. Help me to make this right.* The rage surged within her, her vision tinting red and her hands curling into fists. She fought it down with an effort. Blind anger would not help her figure a way out of this.

BOOM.

The vault lurched, the bronze door canting suddenly, buckling at the corners. The spiderweb of cracks in the timber above it exploded with a roar, and Heloise shut her eyes as wood and stone splinters sprayed across her, filling her mouth with dust. The machine rocked left and right as beams fell on it, each heavier than the last. She ducked her head, her ears ringing as the blows sounded against the metal.

Cold air rushed in, chill raindrops pattered against her face. *It smashed through the roof.* Then there was a rending roar, as if the whole workshop were crying out, and suddenly the machine was pressing down on her, harder and harder. Her legs popped off the ledge, dropping into the machine's legs, scraping against the metal frame all the way down. Her right leg slashed against a rivet, digging a deep furrow in her skin. The machine lurched to one side, groaning, and suddenly her right foot had reached the bottom of the machine's leg, slamming against the buckled strap hard enough to make Heloise's teeth click together.

One moment, her eyes were level with the machine's gorget, and the next she was looking out the helmet's eye-slit. The crown of the helmet rang against her head and she saw stars, felt something hot and sticky run into her eyes.

She screamed, blinked the red out of her eyes, coughed out dust and swallowed blood. Her leg sang and her ears rang and her head felt like it had been split open. She shook her head, though the move hurt so badly that she retched, hanging by the chest strap. She was hurt, but she was alive.

The machine was canted sideways. The collapsing roof had crushed it into a bent posture, making it a metal hunchback. The cold rain on her face cleared her head a bit, stinging as the water ran into her wounds. She would be all right, she just had to—

There was a sound of wood breaking and something huge and heavy slammed into the machine's right arm. The metal groaned, protested, and sheared off, the frame crushing down on her hand.

The metal closed like a vise, making the sleeve into a tapering tunnel, narrowing to a tight point at the machine's metal elbow.

And her flesh hand.

Heloise lost time. One moment, she was in the worst pain of her life, her hand ground to powder, the metal shards of the machine piercing her arm, her face, dragging down her side. The next, she was dimly aware of waking up, as if from a long sleep. Vomit was drying on the front of her shift. Her head throbbed so that even the faint light reaching her through the storm-addled sky was an agony. She closed her eyes, but it didn't help. Her arm, her side, and her leg felt as if they'd been flayed. Her hand hurt least of all, until she tried to wiggle her fingers, producing a white flare of agony that nearly made her faint again. She sawed her head to the right, looking down the tapering metal tunnel that was the machine's arm. The frame had been crushed almost to a point before being ripped off at the elbow, leaving a circle of splayed, jagged ends, like the petals of some sharp metal flower, just about to open.

Her hand was trapped inside, little more than a red bag of shattered bones. The stretched surface of the skin was swollen, purple, weeping blood. She could feel the tiny bones grinding against one another when she'd wiggled what remained of her fingers. The machine's elbow strap was pulled tight across the crushed mess.

She expected to be sick again, or to faint, but her mangled hand felt far away now, someone else's limb. She looked back at her left arm, whole, the skin strangely pale and smooth after looking at the ruin of her right hand. Looking at this half of her, she could almost believe she was all right.

Am I going to die? She was amazed to find that the thought didn't scare her, only filled her with a deep sadness at the thought that she would never see her parents or Basina again.

Basina.

She was likely outside the ruin of the broken bronze door, with the devil. She would need help. The thought made Heloise twitch, her body jerking with a need to escape the machine, but the agony in her hand, leg, and head answered that in an instant. She was stuck. She would have to rip her right hand free to get out, and that would be the end of her.

The stink of seethestone suddenly rose in her nostrils, making her sneeze. She heard a soft sizzling and turned her head to the salted cloth bag. Some rain must have spattered down inside, activating the seethestone. The bag began to dance gently on its drawstrings, swelling with the gas building inside. Heloise's heart sank. If only the seethestone were in the engine, instead of in the bag. Then she could . . .

Heloise turned her head so sharply that she felt the muscles in her neck protest. Pain lanced through her skull, but she ignored it, swallowed the sickness that rose in her throat. *You will not faint you will not faint you will not faint.*

The tube leading to the engine canister was within her reach. The collapsing frame had crushed it halfway shut, but if she pushed hard enough, she could probably get some of the stone in there. *Praise the Emperor. Thank you.*

She slid her good left arm out from the strap, reached across and thrust her hand into the bag. The stone, normally dry and waxy, felt slimy now. It bubbled against her palm as she seized it, tickling her skin. Reminding her of Twitch's nose against her hand. She pushed the thought away. *Get it into the engine before it's spent.*

She lifted her hand out of the bag, and the tickling became burning. She brought her hand to the tube, and the burning became agony. It felt as if her palm and fingers were steeped in fire. As if the seethestone were an army of stinging insects savaging the skin beneath. She screamed, her hand shaking, the slick chunk of stone threatening to slide out of her palm.

She thought of Basina, of her father, of the Tinkers. She thought of her father running from the Maior's privy, of Clodio slumping to the ground. All of it because of her. *You will not drop it. I don't care if your hand burns off.*

She raised her hand to the chute, pinning the stone against it. It was too large to fit in the half-crushed opening, and it slid against the metal, threatening to pop out of her grip. She pushed harder, and the agony increased. She felt her skin sloughing off in patches as the stone's slick, burning edges dug in. She loosened her grip, got her palm firmly behind the stone, and pushed.

Heloise could hear a screaming, high and long, impossibly loud. It took her a moment to realize it was herself. The pressure against her palm suddenly ceased, and she heard the stone tumbling down the chute, rattling against the metal sides, until it gave a final clang against the engine's bottom, splashing into the pooling rainwater.

Heloise screamed again, this time in triumph, and hauled on the handle swinging the canister lid shut. Her burned flesh sang, and she turned her eyes away, not wanting to see, but she couldn't help but catch a glimpse of her hand, the surface pink and bubbling.

A roaring rose in her ears, and at first she thought it was the devil, finally through the roof and after her, but then the frame around her began to rattle, and she realized it was the war-machine coughing to life, coming awake around her.

The machine was half-crushed, bent at the waist, and missing half its right arm. But it was still upright. Like its driver, crippled, but alive.

She turned and put her burned hand back into the machine's left sleeve, slid it behind the looped strap there. It hurt, but not as badly as when she'd clutched the seethestone, and the pain troubled her less, now that there was so much of it, and everywhere at once. She gave the strap a tug, holding her breath, not daring to believe that she could drive a tinker-made engine of war.

The machine's left arm jerked up, sliding the shield across the frame's chest, covering the eye slit. Heloise lowered her arm and the machine's arm lowered with it, until the shield's top edge was just below her eyes. Her left foot still dangled over empty space, but she wiggled her right one under the foot strap, gave it an experimental tug. The machine's right foot trembled in response.

And suddenly, the pain didn't matter. She was Heloise the girl no longer. She was taller than a man grown, taller than Barnard, even. The falling roof had crushed the machine small enough for her limbs to reach, for her to drive it. It was a piece of luck so great it had to be divine.

Emperor, if this is a sign, I see it. I know this is my fault. Help me to make it right. She raised her shoulder, felt the strap pull in response, and the engine driving the rods along the machine's frame. The shield came up, a solid piece of metal that two men couldn't lift on their own. She glanced down at her ruined hand, sprouting from the machine's broken arm, the red stigma at the center of a sharp, jagged metal flower. It was a tiny weapon compared to the hammer Barnard had been trying to mount, but it would have to do.

She lifted her right foot, then let it drop, turned her body so it tugged the chest strap on one side. The war-machine responded, limping, lurching, spinning until it faced the battered bronze door, askew in the splintered frame. Her wounds screamed, her ruined hands crying out, but she welcomed the pain now. She was the Emperor's Hand. He had hurt her to give her the means to save her village, to save Basina and her parents.

The machine had been crushed to one side, allowing her right foot to reach the strap that controlled the right leg. But her left foot was unable to reach its strap, and so the machine's left leg was limp and dragging. She took a limping, shuddering step and the war-machine limped with her. Within moments, her armpits and chest were rubbed raw by the leather chest strap. Each step bounced her, dragging the shoulder straps down, making the arms swing and the entire machine shudder and lurch.

She reached the door and punched out with her good hand. The shield's corner swept up, smashing into the bronze with a clang louder than the bell in the steeple of the Emperor's shrine. The door spun away as if it were made of wood, out into the workshop beyond.

Heloise stepped out and into the light.

The workshop was destroyed. Tables, tools, and anvils were scattered on the dirt floor, soaking in the gray water from overturned quenching buckets mixing with the clear droplets of rain. The devil had smashed through the roof from the workshop entrance all the way through the vault, so that what had once been a forging floor was now an amphitheater, open to the air. The crucible bubbled and spat, protesting the cool water falling into it from the spitting sky. The devil stood, snarling and hissing, reaching for the vault with a clawed hand.

Barnard stood before it, swinging his giant forge hammer in both his hands, knocking it into the monster's fist, driving it back. Gunnar was at his side, his gloved hand holding a long rod of stock iron, its end still glowing cherry red from the forging fire, casting sparks at the touch of the rain. He thrust it into the devil's face, forcing it back a step, hissing and snapping. Its mouth opened impossibly wide, the jaw unhinging like a snake's. Triple rows of sharp black teeth shone wetly, a cluster of tiny black tongues waved like a field of malevolent flowers.

It gave another raptor shriek, so loud that Heloise felt her ears ring, but it was scant pain compared to her hands, her leg, her side.

And now, when she needed it, her terror gave way to anger. Hot and heedless, as it had been on the road to Hammersdown, when all of this had begun. Heloise screamed back, so loud and so long that her throat felt raw. She took another step, the machine shaking as she advanced, the one working leg kicking through the rubble.

The devil turned, hissed, eye clusters narrowing as it focused on her. The fear kindled in her belly again, making her limbs weak. The creature crouched, fanning its six arms out, ignoring Barnard and his son as it turned to face her.

Beneath the crook of its lowest arm, Heloise could see Basina, her dress filthy and soaked, her eyes lit with terror. She held a wood axe in her hands, far too short to be of much use against the monster, but she advanced on it anyway.

Basina. Clearly terrified, moving forward anyway.

Heloise smelled rotting wood, the odor of the kind of life that is happy where there is too much water and not enough light. The monster opened its oblong mouth, waving black tongues vibrating a hiss.

"Come on!" Heloise screamed, rolling her shoulder, banging the shield's edge into the war-machine's metal chest, raising a clang that echoed around them.

The devil shouted back.

Heloise charged.

She got the shield up just in time to block the devil's first punch. The heavy fist was followed by a second, then a third, so powerful that it battered the shield's edge back against the driver's cage, making it shake around her. She rolled her opposite shoulder, trying to bring her right arm to bear, but the jagged metal shards were too short to reach around the shield and strike the devil on the other side. She would have to turn her body sideways, coming out from behind the shield's protection, to make a good strike.

Or she could hold it fast until the Tinkers brought it down.

"Basina!" Her cry turned into a shriek as the devil's face appeared over the top of her shield, mouth snapping at her, spraying the top of her head with stinking spit. It punched again and again, driving the war-machine back, but Heloise launched herself forward, and the machine moved with her, throwing itself behind the shield, pushing against it. Each blow made the frame rattle and her wounds sing. Her pulped hand screamed as the leather strap jerked against it, threatening to make her faint again, but Heloise hung on. The Tinkers had done their work well. The shield was good, stout metal, strongly made. It would hold.

The devil seemed to realize this too, wrapped two hands over the top of the shield, pressed down, trying to make room to push its head inside the driver's cage. It growled, snarled, but blessedly did not shriek. In the tight space inside the machine, Heloise was sure the cry would have deafened her. Having it so close was bad enough. The stink of rot, of boggy ground, was so powerful that she gagged.

Heloise felt the shield tremble, heard the sound of grinding metal. The devil snarled and pushed harder. Slowly, the shield began to drop. Heloise screamed, pushing her shoulder up, felt the strap cinch tight around her, straining against the skin. The pain was so great that she felt sick again. The tinker-engine roared, belched a great cloud of smoke. The metal groaned as it strained against the monster's weight.

The shield stopped, shivered, and slowly began to rise.

The devil growled and pushed harder, and the shield ground to a halt. Heloise felt the machine straining, could hear the bellow of the engine behind her. She pushed against the strap with everything she had. She could feel the charred skin on her burned hand slide away against the leather strap, grit her teeth to keep from vomiting. Nothing. The shield would not move. Heloise and the devil pushed against one another for a moment, neither able to gain the advantage.

At last the devil took a step back, putting another hand on the shield's edge, pulling and pushing at the same time. The shield trembled. *You can't do this forever. Sooner or later, it's going to get the shield out of the way. You have to do something.*

She pulled against the chest strap and the machine bent lower, the shield's corner sinking. There was a sickening moment of terror as the metal moved out of the way of the driver's cage and the devil seized the chance, mouth yawning wide, sharp teeth racing toward her.

Heloise drove off with her right foot and straightened, hammering the shield up under the devil's chin. Its teeth clicked together, neck snapping back. It reeled, three of its arms pinwheeling as it tried to keep its balance. Heloise gave a triumphant shout. She couldn't see the Tinkers, but it didn't matter. Even with the machine bent and twisted, she didn't need them. Perhaps it was because the Emperor had blessed her. Perhaps it was simply dumb luck. Either way, she was winning.

The devil stumbled back, flailed with two of its arms, and grasped the machine's shoulders. Its weight came down on its ankle and it collapsed, turning sideways as it fell.

Heloise felt its weight dragging at the machine. She had thought that the metal frame was strong enough to carry anything, but the devil was huge, and strain as she might against the straps, its giant body pulled the machine down with it. Heloise felt the world upend, the horizon became the devil's chest, and the machine toppled forward.

The devil rolled as they came down, throwing its strength into its shoulders, flipping the war-machine onto its back and rolling on top of it. The metal groaned and shook, and Heloise rattled inside it, her vision filling with stars as her head snapped back and forth. Her back slammed against the frame hard enough to shake her teeth and knock the breath from her. She lay, gasping, trying to move her arms as the devil shook its head, stalked eyes swiveling back toward her, pushing itself up on its fists and making ready to reach for her.

She heard a shout, and Barnard appeared at the devil's side. He swung his hammer, knocking the devil's arm away. The devil turned toward him, hissing. Gunnar joined his father, stabbing at its eye, but the iron bar had cooled now, and the gray metal merely raked across its cheek.

The devil shrieked and swept an arm back, catching Gunnar and Barnard across the chest, sending them sprawling across the ruined workshop, weapons flying from their hands.

No. Heloise had precious little time to worry about the Tinkers, for the devil had turned back to her, was leaning in.

Heloise pulled on her pulped right hand, desperate to free it from the metal sleeve, to escape from the machine before the devil could hurt her. But she still couldn't catch her breath, and even if she could, the strap around her hand held fast, so that her struggles only made the broken metal arm flail uselessly against the devil's weight. The pain was so great that she was certain that to rip her hand free would kill her.

The devil didn't bother with biting this time. It reached a single finger inside the driver's cage, the claw on the end long and sharp as any knife.

There was a shout and Basina appeared over the devil's shoulder, springing lightly up its back, the axe flashing in her hands. "Get off her!" she shouted, and swung the axe as if she were splitting a log, down at the devil's neck.

The devil screamed, so high and piercing that Heloise's eyes watered, the pain in her ears rising and rising until at last all sound fled and there was only a ringing, high and tinny and sounding like it came from a long way off. The devil twisted, jerking its head up and back, and the axe head turned as it struck, the edge finding no purchase, arcing out and down. It cut, but not deep enough. Black blood showered Heloise, mixing with her own, the stink of it leaving her retching, still barely able to breathe.

The devil shrieked silently. All Heloise could hear was the high ringing in her ears. Basina's face was milk pale, eyes wide. She raised the axe for another blow, but much too late. The devil was already rising, jerking its shoulder back, throwing her off. Basina sprang clear, tumbling beneath a swiping claw that tore a rent in her dress.

Basina tumbled out of view and the devil turned to follow, opening its mouth and shrieking again.

Move. This is your chance. Get up, get up, get up! Heloise sucked in air, her lungs inflating painfully. Some of the black blood dripped into her mouth and she sputtered, turning her head and spitting down her shoulder. Her body ached and her limbs felt weak, but she thought she could move them. She pushed on one side of the chest strap, pulled up with her good shoulder. The machine groaned and clanked and the arm answered her sluggishly, but at last she felt the shield dig into the ground beneath her and push her up to a sitting position.

Barnard and Gunnar lay in the wreckage, still. The devil hunched, spread its arms, and shrieked again, took a step toward Basina. Heloise could hear it now, faintly, the ringing fading and the sounds of the world rushing back. Basina brandished her axe and screamed back, but where the devil's scream was angry, Basina's was frightened.

Heloise could see the devil knew this. It growled low in its throat, a sound like a pack of dogs circling.

The devil twitched. Basina turned and ran.

Heloise pulled on the foot strap, desperately trying to get the machine's feet under it, unable to tear her eyes away.

The devil stalked slowly after Basina, enjoying the chase. The machine kicked in the dirt, succeeding only in digging great furrows in the muck. Her wounds sang out with every movement, but it was an old song to her now, sung so many times that she knew the words by heart. She was good at hurting.

Heloise gave up on kicking and sawed her chest against the strap. The machine's shoulders moved in time and she pushed harder, trying to rock the machine onto its knees. Desperation was supposed to give people strength, but it only made her arms and legs feel weak, heavy. It only made it hard to breathe.

"Come on, come on," she whispered. Not Basina. Not her love. She couldn't let this happen.

At last, the rocking carried the machine over, and she was falling forward so fast that she only just managed to catch herself with the shield's corner. She pushed again, felt the weight of the machine resisting her.

She pushed harder. Her teeth ground together. Slowly, the machine began to rise. Too slowly. Harder. Blood pounded in her ears. She felt a vein burst in her nose, blood trickling down onto her lip. Somewhere, just ahead of her, the devil was running down her best friend. The love of her life.

She gave a final shout and punched out with the shield, knocking the machine up and back onto its feet. She staggered back a step, steadied herself. At first, she couldn't believe she was up, but there was Basina, the devil herding her back.

The devil didn't notice her. Basina did.

Maybe Basina was exhausted, or mad with fear. She doubled back toward the war-machine, bringing her closer to the devil, which gave up its stalking and struck.

The devil brought a fist down. Basina jumped aside, swung the axe one-handed, the head rebounding off the devil's armored hand. The devil screamed, pulled the hand away. The movement dragged the axe from Basina's grip, sent it spinning into the air.

Basina turned again and ran in the opposite direction, eyes wide. The devil glanced at its hand, shrieked, and followed.

"Basina!" Heloise yelled, limping after them. The devil's legs were twice as long as Basina was tall. There was no patient stalking now, no low growling, only the quiet speed of revenge.

Heloise pursued the devil with everything she had. She panted, lungs burning. Her leg ached with the effort of yanking her foot up and kicking it down again, feeling the metal leg move in response, dragging the limp one behind. The leather strap had chewed through her dress, through the skin of her armpits, wet with her blood, singing in pain with every movement. She felt the machine's bent posture keenly now, its staggering limp, even as the devil's broad back grew in her vision. She had to go faster. She had to get there before it could hurt Basina.

Basina ran and the devil followed, just behind her now, raising a huge hand.

"No!" Heloise shouted, she yanked her good foot up, trying to stretch the leg further, faster. The machine took a great, lumbering stride, the bent cage unbalancing it, sending it teetering sideways. She reached out with the shield, flailing for the devil's back.

She was falling sideways. The weight of the shield was an anchor now, dragging her earthward. She yanked her foot up and slammed it back down again, hoping the motion would right her, succeeding only in splashing the mud that the rain had made of the workshop floor. She felt the machine's balance drift past the point of no return. The devil's back slid sideways past her.

The devil's hand came down, smashing Basina to the ground.

Rage swamped her, banished pain, banished fatigue, her vision narrowing to a tunnel that showed only the devil's back passing by. Heloise screamed, punched out with the shield arm, felt the shield's corner brush the devil's back, hook the monster's shoulder blade, take the machine's weight. The machine swung around, rolling until it faced the devil's side, the ruined right arm pointing toward its heart.

Heloise rolled her shoulder and the machine's huge arm pulled on the shield. The corner held fast, yanking the machine in, driving the jagged metal remains of the broken metal arm deep into the devil's side.

She felt the sharp metal go in, deeper than she'd thought possible. The black blood covered her arm, dripped into the cage, the stink familiar now, bothering her less.

She felt her right arm now, puncturing through the devil's skin and stabbing deep into it. She could feel the ribs briefly resist, but they were no match for the strength of the tinker-engine, and she felt them crunch under the sharp metal, hungrily delving deeper.

The devil didn't scream. It straightened, head swiveling toward her. She could look at its face now, the thin slice of a mouth, the uneven slits for nostrils, the clustered stalks of its white eyes.

Heloise stared into them, pushing her hatred into her look. She wanted it to see how she felt. "You killed Clodio," she said.

The eye stalks moved closer together, until they formed an almost one great eye. The growling stopped. Was it listening to her? Did it recognize her? She hoped so. She hoped it could hear her.

She whispered as she pushed the broken metal deeper in. "Kill you." It became a growl.

Below them, Basina kicked, moaned. The devil's mouth opened, the tongues reaching out, black flowers blooming on long stems. The inside was gray, wet, stinking of swamps.

The stalked eyes glowed, turned in circles. The mouth snapped shut, and Heloise felt the monster slough sideways. The machine's weight added to the momentum, and they were falling again. There was a rush of wind, then a crash, and Heloise knew she was down. The impact wasn't as bad this time, or at least Heloise didn't notice it. She only knew that she had to get up, because it still might be alive, because she had to finish this.

She felt the engine on the machine's back shudder. It belched a great gout of seethestone smoke. The metal shook and groaned, and then the engine gave a final cough and died. The strength went out of the war-machine, and it lay slack, wrapped around the devil's body, embraced like lovers.

Heloise waited for the devil to stir, to rise and tear her apart. She couldn't stop it. She had no more strength in her. She had failed too badly, too often.

But the devil didn't move, and the thought of Basina lying wounded would not let her be.

She struggled against the straps, but they held her fast. The agony in her right hand again nearly made her faint, and she finally stopped trying, instead swinging her head up and past the crushed frame to see if the devil still breathed.

The thing's eyes were gray. There was no sound of the wet breathing now. The black tongues dripped blacker blood from the corner of its open mouth. Its head was turned to the side, hanging on its thick neck.

It was dead.

She had done it.

Basina.

She craned her neck, finally let herself see her best friend. She gasped.

Basina's body was crushed flat from just above her hips to the tops of her knees. Her blood soaked all around her, the blue ropes of her guts spilled out into the mud. She stank like a midden baking in the sun.

She was smiling. "You killed it?"

"Yes." Heloise realized she was crying. "I killed it."

"That's good," Basina whispered. Her face was as white as the devil's eyes. Blood bubbled at the corners of her mouth. "I knew you would."

I will never let anyone hurt you, Heloise had said to her. In her heart, it had been an oath. "Basina, I'm sorry. I'm so sorry."

"Don't be sorry," she said. "I lost my axe."

Heloise cried, cuffed tears from her eyes. "Basina, I'm sorry. I'm sorry for everything. But I love you and I tried to save you and I didn't mean for any of this . . ."

"It's all right." Basina seemed to be reaching for something, but all she could do was wiggle her fingers in the mud. Even that small effort melted her smile, and her eyes went sad. She coughed blood. The pain in Basina's face went away, her eyes lost focus, she looked confused. "I'm sorry. I'm not brave like you, Heloise."

"Yes, you are, Basina. You are brave. And you just have to be brave a little longer, you just have to hold on. I'm going to get out of this machine and get Deuteria. She can fix you." She looked back down the machine's right arm, trying to see if there was some way she could slip her hand free. She struggled against the straps, nearly fainted from the pain. "Basina? Basina, don't go to sleep! Talk to me! Basina?"

But Basina didn't answer, and when Heloise looked back to her, she knew she was gone.

14

PALANTINE

Do not weep for your dead. For, if they have lived by my
   Writ,
They are not gone, but stand in splendor beside the
   Throne.
They lend their strength to mine, and together watch o'er
   you and yours,
Unto your last day, when they will greet you.
And in this way, the ranks of the righteous ever swell,
And assure that hell will one day be laid low, forever.
Have faith, and hold fast, and thou shalt know peace at
   the end.
                    —*Writ. Imp. XXX. 5*

Heloise rose up through the layers of darkness, her senses return-ing slowly. Her hands, her side, her leg throbbed, the pain mad-dening. Beyond it, there was nothing. It was as if all else in her had been scoured away in the fight with the devil, leaving a crea-ture whose sole purpose was to hurt.

She was lying on wood, the slightly uneven surface of the boards digging into her shoulders. Her head rested on a bag of grain.

Voices were speaking around her, deep and hard. Men talking in tones she knew were used for important things.

She heard angry sobbing. Barnard.

"Are you certain you can go on with this?" Sigir.

The sob choked off, swallowed.

"Barnard, you don't have . . ." Her father's voice.

"I. Will. Do. It." It was certainly the tinker's voice, but with an edge to it that chilled Heloise.

"There should be time for grief," the Maior said. "We should be burying our dead and—"

"We are wasting time," Barnard said.

"What can we do?" Her father's voice. "Will there be more?"

"Are you speaking of the devil, Samson?" Sigir asked. "Devils are the least of our worries now. We would be fortunate indeed if a tide from hell were to wash across us now. It would be quicker. Cleaner."

"How can you say—"

"There is no time!" Sigir's voice was loud with anger that Heloise knew covered fear. "The Order is regrouping even as we speak. If we are lucky, they will send for reinforcements. If not, they will come upon us as we are. We have no wizard to defend us now."

"We have better than a wizard," Barnard said. "We have a Palantine."

"That is my daughter," Samson snarled. "She is just a little girl and she is hurt and—"

"She killed a devil," Barnard said. "She killed a devil and she lives."

"Your war-machine killed a devil!" Samson shouted. "She's just—"

"Your daughter is alive!" Barnard roared. His voice was strained, choked with tears. He sounded exhausted. He sounded mad. "She stood against a devil and lived. Why would that be, save for the Emperor's will? What little girl could drive a war-machine, broken as it was? She is a Sainted Palantine! She will protect us!" Heloise could hear Gunnar and Guntar whispering to their father, trying to calm him.

"Barnard." Samson's voice was gentle. "I am sorry for Basina. I truly am."

Basina. Grief welled up in Heloise's chest. Her best friend was dead. She hadn't been able to save her.

Barnard made a strangled sound. "Why should my daughter die and yours live? It is the Emperor's will. She is a Palantine."

"All things are the Emperor's will," Samson said. "Good and bad alike. I am sorry for your loss. Basina was like a daughter to me, I feel it too. But it doesn't make Heloise anything more than a wounded child."

"Sainted Palantine or no," Sigir said. "She is too weak to stand now, let alone drive a war-machine. The Order is coming. They will call on one of the Frogging Clans to run their cordon. We will be Knit, Samson. We will be Knit in a fortnight at the most."

Sigir's words brought a silence so heavy that it blotted out even the normal sounds of the wind sighing against the roof, of birds nesting in the eves.

"What do we do?" her father asked.

"We prepare as best we can," Sigir answered, "and we make what defenses we may. If we're to have any chance of surviving at all, we'll need to take good ground, strike at the Order from ambush."

"The ranger," her father said. "I wish he was still with us. He knew the land."

But he can't be here, Heloise thought, *because he became a portal into hell. And I knew he was a wizard and didn't stop him.*

"The boys have done a fair bit of ranging," Barnard said. "Guntar is a good tracker. I'll set him to find which way the Order went. We'll need to look along the road to Lyse. Might be there's a spot they won't expect us coming out of."

"I know just the spot," Guntar said. "I'm sure I can find it again."

"Be quick," Sigir said. "We are already out of time."

The Maior paused, then spoke again. "We will raise the whole village. Everyone, man or woman, old enough to walk or young enough to hold a spear. We will not get another chance should we lose. I will not see my people butchered like . . ." He trailed off, choking on his words.

"Like Hammersdown," Heloise said, her voice a dry croak. "Like Alna and Jaran. Like Austre. And all the rest we killed." Her throat felt as if she'd swallowed sand. She had promised Basina she would protect her, and she had failed. Basina whom she loved. Basina who had saved her. She had to make that right.

She opened her eyes, and this time light came in, revealing the thick, dark beams of the gathering hall ceiling. She began to sit up, reaching behind her to push off what turned out to be one of the hall's long benches. Her hand somehow missed the wood, and she slumped against the table's edge.

"Easy, now," Deuteria said from behind her. Heloise could feel the herber reaching for her.

Samson got there first, lifting her up. "Heloise, you need to rest."

Heloise looked down. Deuteria had covered her in soft linen smeared with something that stained the fabric dirty yellow. Even with the medicine, her body burned as if a fire were lit within it, and at the same time, a shivering cold. Her head throbbed.

But all thought of fever and pain disappeared as her eyes fell on her right hand. It no longer pained her, in fact she could still feel her wiggling fingers. But they were phantoms. Linen was wrapped tightly around the stump of her wrist, stained a deep brown.

Her hand was gone.

"We could not save it," Deuteria said. "I am sorry."

"I will make you another," Barnard said in his mad voice. "A tinker-engine worthy of a Palantine."

Heloise looked into Barnard's eyes, and the grief there nearly overwhelmed her. Whatever Basina's loss was to her, it was at least the same to him. Gunnar and Guntar were weeping, but she caught their sidelong glances at her, saw the awe in their eyes. But she couldn't let them make her something she was not.

"I am no Palantine," she said.

"You are," Barnard croaked. "You have to be." *He needs me to be, otherwise, why did Basina die?*

She stared at the stump of her wrist. She could feel her hand, had to force herself to believe it wasn't there. She shook her head. It was nothing. Basina was dead, but Barnard and his family were alive. If there was any reason why Heloise was still here, that had to be it.

"You heard the Maior," Heloise said, "there is no time to rest."

"There is for you," her father said. "You will need your strength for what's ahead."

"That's not true," Heloise said. "You know I won't heal enough to do anything before the Order comes."

She heard Deuteria suck in her breath, saw her father's face darken.

"No." Sigir sounded exhausted. "She's right, Samson. She's no longer a child. Hasn't been for some time now."

"Child or no," Samson said. "She cannot fight."

"You will live, Heloise," Deuteria added, "and you may recover, in time. But there is nothing for it now but what healing sleep will bring. We must hope the wounds don't sour, and the best chance you have of preventing this is to be away from anything that might soil you. We will bring you food and drink. You must stay still, on this bench. You must not do anything that will anger the wounds. You must sleep."

"No," Heloise said. "You just said you would arm every man, woman, and child. You said we wouldn't get a second chance."

"You are too wounded!" Samson said.

"So, you want me to die on my back? In this hall?" Heloise asked.

"The Palantine wants to fight," Barnard said, "she must fight. The Emperor will be with us if she does."

Samson swallowed, slowed his breathing, but his voice still shook. "Barnard, I know you are grieving. We all mourn Basina's loss. But Heloise is lucky to be alive and I will not see her sicken and die because—"

"She will not sicken and she will not die." Barnard's voice was as certain as steel. "She is a Palantine."

Samson's face purpled. "Will you stop putting notions into her head? Weren't you listening to the herber?"

"I was, and it doesn't matter," Barnard said. "The Emperor has put his hand on her. Nothing can harm her, and nothing can harm those who stand with her. If we are to live, she must fight."

"She is *not* going to fight. I am her father and I forbid it."

"Enough." Heloise's voice sounded strange, even to her. Deeper, older. Basina was dead. Clodio was dead. Heloise couldn't lie here on a table and try to get well, no matter what her father said. "I will fight."

"You can't!" Samson shouted.

"She killed a devil," Barnard said. "She can do anything."

"She had your machine! And it is destroyed now!"

Heloise looked at her father, saw the pleading in his eyes. She knew how terrified he must be, desperate to help someone he loved, unable to. She knew exactly how he felt.

Which was why she had to do this.

"Master Tinker," she said, "the second war-machine, can you finish it? Can you make it fit me?" She had killed a devil in a bent and crippled machine. Her heart thrilled at the thought of what she could do in one that was whole.

"I can, your eminence," Barnard said, bowing his head. "I can and I will. I will work without eating, without sleeping, until it is done. It will be ready before the Order arrives, I swear it in the shadow of the Throne."

"Please don't call me that," she said. "That's what they call Sojourners."

Barnard inclined his head, which frightened her even more than his use of the title. Barnard Tinker, the mountain of a man who had been all but a second father to her, following her orders as if she were a lord.

"Heloise," Samson pleaded. "Please. Please, don't do this."

"I'm sorry, Father. I must."

"Maior," Samson rasped, desperate. "I am her father. Forbid this. Call the Tipstaffs, help me tie her down."

Barnard's voice went dark. "I will kill the man who tries."

His sons stood at his shoulders, each nearly as big as him. Guntar crossed his arms across his chest. "She is a Palantine, as Father says. She wants to fight. She fights."

Heloise saw the tension crackling between her father and the Tinkers. Sigir looked back and forth between them, lips moving, saying nothing. She had to stop this. It would be hard enough to fight the Order without fighting among themselves.

"She said she is no—" Samson began.

"If killing a devil doesn't make me a Palantine," Heloise said, "it at least makes me a woman grown. A woman grown with no husband makes her own decisions, and this is mine."

"Heloise." Samson cradled his head in his hand.

"I killed a devil," Heloise said. Palantine or no, that much was true. Until she was married, a father had the right to refuse a girl anything. She had to be something more.

Barnard grunted and turned to the hall doors. "Let them in," he said to his sons. The Tinker boys threw the doors wide.

A knot of villagers stood outside, staring at the table, awe in their eyes.

Heloise's mouth went dry. She hadn't thought that the village might be listening. It seemed a smaller thing to claim a Palantine's accolade in front of those she knew best, but now she had lied to the whole village.

"Did you hear?" Barnard called to them. "Did you hear her words?"

The villagers dipped their heads and bowed deeply, averting their eyes. "Heloise Devil-Slayer," Danad murmured. "Palantine, Hand of the Emperor, bless us."

Heloise gaped, struggling for something to say. She *had* slain a devil, but it didn't make her the hand of anything, and she couldn't bless anyone. She'd said what she did to stop her father and Barnard from fighting, to ensure she'd have a chance to fight. A few of the children looked at her from under their hair, but the rest kept their eyes firmly on the ground, as if they were addressing a lord, or a member of the Order. "Hand of the Emperor," some of them said. Others said, "Palantine."

"She drove a war-machine to slay the devil," Barnard said. "She will drive another when we stand against the Order."

Sald Grower and Poch Drover alone did not bow. Sald's cheeks were red, but he met Barnard's fanatic gaze evenly. "Master Tinker, we all love Heloise, and thank the Emperor she lives. But that doesn't mean she's the one to put in a war-engine. That's for a man grown to drive."

"Are you blind?" Gunnar shouted at him. "She killed a devil. Go back up to our workshop and you will see it."

"We've seen it," Poch spoke to Sigir. "It was the machine that killed the devil. That don't make her a Palantine."

And then everyone was shouting at once, until Heloise couldn't tell one voice from the other, and Sigir was shouting for everyone to be quiet.

"You're right!" Barnard's voice cut through the throng. "She is no Palatine. They are legends, revered for their place in the grave. She is real. She is breathing. All the Palantines died. She lives. She is something more. Something greater."

The crowd began to shout again, but Barnard shouted over them. "When the Order came to kill us, it wasn't you who turned them back. It was an old man, and a ranger besides. And when a devil came among us, it wasn't you who fought it, it was two little girls. My Basina fell. How else could Heloise live? Against such a monster? How else but the Emperor's divine Hand?"

"It was your machine," Poch said.

"The machine alone could not be driven by a girl of sixteen winters. The Emperor crushed it to fit her."

"Maybe it was the Emperor's Hand," Sald said, "and maybe it was dumb luck. We got one chance against the Order, do you want to risk putting a child in charge of the one thing that could save us? This isn't a game!"

"That machine is mine," Barnard growled, "and I will permit no one to drive it but Heloise Factor."

"Barnard," Sald began.

"Do you think I don't suspect?" Barnard's voice was little more than an animal growl. "You and Poch both spoke against Samson when Sigir decided we would hide him. And the Pilgrims came, twice. Once, right to my workshop and my vault, and the second time, just after Heloise had fled from our protection. How convenient. I wonder why . . ."

"Barnard!" Sigir shouted. "Enough. You have no proof."

Sald's cheeks reddened and his eyes narrowed. "Bald lies to throw us off the matter at hand. That machine is not for—"

"If you want it," Guntar cut him off, "come and take it." Guntar was not yet full grown, but he was a big boy regardless.

Gunnar stepped up beside his brother, red-faced. "Best me, Master Grower. Open hands. Blow for blow. You can have the first strike. If I fall, you may put who you like in that machine. If you lose, I swear in the shadow of the Throne that I will kill you."

No one moved.

"Well?" Guntar shouted. "Are you going to step up, or are you going to stand there?"

Silence. Sald looked at his feet, his jaw working silently.

"Only Heloise," Barnard said. "Devil-Slayer. Palantine. Our own."

The reverence in his voice made her more frightened, more alone in that moment than she'd ever felt in her life. Her need for her father was sudden and desperate. She wanted nothing more than to run to his arms, to feel him stroke her hair and tell her he loved her. She had lost so much so quickly, peace, safety, Clodio, Basina, her hand.

But she knew that once her father put his arms around her, she would never be free of them. She hadn't been able to save Basina, or Clodio, and if she was ever going to make that right, she couldn't let that happen.

"Look at her," Poch shouted. "She's half-dead!"

"She is the Emperor's Own, and beyond death," Barnard answered. "In the machine, her body will match her heart. She will be strong enough to stand against a Pilgrim and throw him down."

More than a Pilgrim, Heloise knew. More than two or three of them, at least.

But the thought didn't make her feel brave or strong. Instead, she thought of Basina, of how she looked before the light had faded from her eyes. The villagers muttered, turned away. Sald and Poch looked as if they would say more, but they thought better of it.

"I'm frightened," Heloise whispered, more to herself than anyone else.

But Barnard turned to her, and for a moment, the madness left his voice. "We all are. Fear's a deadly thing, Heloise. It can drain a person of all their strength, make them weak before their enemies. That's how we were until you showed us different. But we see now, and we are not afraid anymore, so long as you are with us. You are Heloise the Devil-Slayer. Never forget that."

She looked back at her father, eyes red-rimmed, wringing his hands. *Your father's no great harbor from a wicked world,* he had said. How badly she wished that wasn't true. Once she climbed inside the new machine, he would be lost to her every bit as much as Clodio and Basina.

She turned back to Barnard. He was mad with grief, believed her to be something she wasn't. But he was all she had now. "You'll be with me?"

"While breath remains in me," the huge man said, "I will never leave your side."

He turned to his sons. "Bring the machine here, and my tools. Heloise will rest while we work. She will not move until she must."

Samson came to her side, glaring daggers at Barnard. But he said nothing, held out a bowl of hot soup. "Please," he said. "Palantine or no, you have to eat."

Heloise realized with a start that she was hungry, her stomach a clenched knot that was only now beginning to loosen. At first, she reached for the spoon with her phantom hand, but quickly corrected herself. When she finally lifted the spoon with her good one, her father had to hold the bowl for her. The simple act nearly brought her to tears. *I'm sorry, Papa. Please don't be angry. I have to do this.*

The village watched her eat, as if they were afraid she would vanish the moment they took their eyes off her. Heloise stared back at them between bites, nodded at the ones who tugged their forelocks and looked away.

She was terrified, but she knew that if she seemed brave, they would think she was, and that could make them brave too.

She turned again to Barnard. "Even with the war-machine, it will be a hard fight," she said.

"It will," the giant tinker said.

"And if we win?" she asked.

"We *will* win," he said. "You are—"

"No," Heloise cut him off. "*When* we win. What then?"

Barnard stammered, shook his head. After a moment, he sighed. "Then, things will change."

Heloise thought of Austre, facedown in the mud as her home burned behind her. She thought of the dead woman, dragged in chains down the Hammersdown road, her gray tongue swollen out of her mouth. Heloise knew she was no Palantine, knew that even Barnard's burning faith and his engine were no guarantees of victory. The village had a few veterans, but without arms and armor, they were little more than a rabble.

The fight to come would be hard; victory to be won only by the slimmest chance. But slim was more than none.

·   ·   ·

Outside, the wind picked up, and the first snows of early winter gusted through the hall's open doors. The white flakes swirled for a moment before settling around her feet and melting into the flagstones. Outside, they dusted the boots of the Tinker boys as they trudged up the path to the ruin of their workshop where the war-machine waited.

She was no Palantine. A little girl shouldn't lead an army. This wasn't the way things were supposed to be.

Heloise looked back up at Barnard. "Things will change."

He nodded. "Aye, your eminence. They already have."

And though it seemed a strange thing to do after all that had happened, Heloise smiled.

ACKNOWLEDGMENTS

I've always tried to push the envelope of my writing with each book, but the one you're holding in your hand represents the biggest leap I've ever made. Prior to Tor.com picking this up, I had only ever written hard-edged military novels, and getting someone to believe in my ability to execute with wider range required luck, faith, and a large measure of persistence.

It also required people who believed in me to the degree where they were willing to take a chance. First and foremost is Justin Landon, who contacted me after learning I'd trunked the book after working on it unsuccessfully for three years, and first told me he thought the project had legs. Justin convinced me to revive it, and then did all the necessary hand-holding to bring it to life. It isn't an understatement to say that, without him, this book would still be gathering dust on my hard drive. I also want to thank Irene Gallo and Lee Harris, both of whom were willing to ante up and put money and business clout down behind Justin's belief. Also thanks to Sam Morgan and Lisa Rodgers, who likewise saw merit in the project when no one else did. Thanks also to Kat Howard, who generously donated editorial time for which she deserves to be highly paid.

A very special thanks to Kevin Hearne. I drunkenly confessed to him in a hotel bar that I was getting nowhere with the book. Kevin not only asked me to lay down the plot, but sat there and listened while I (maudlin and slurring) made my way through it. When I was done he said, "I don't know what you're so bummed out about. I think it's awesome. I can't wait to read it, and more importantly, I can't wait for my daughter to read it." I cannot tell you how important those fifteen minutes were for me. Art can be lonely and anxious in equal measure, and you never know when simply clapping someone on the shoulder will make all the difference.

Last, but not least, thanks are due to you, the reader. I wrote this book to prove to myself that I was a Writer with a capital "W," but I also wrote it to prove it to *you*.

Thanks for giving me my shot.

Read on for a sneak peek of the next novel
in the Sacred Throne trilogy

THE QUEEN OF CROWS

Available October 2018

I

THE ARMORED GIRL

Heloise wasn't a small girl, but she'd never been a big one either. *Right in the middle,* her father had always said, *and perfect that way,* her mother was quick to add.

The war-machine made her a giant, a steel-monster puffing seethestone smoke into the gray sky. One of the machine's metal fists was hidden behind a shield heavy enough to crush an ox's skull even without the engine's brutal strength. The other fist was empty, but no less deadly for it, an unforgiving bludgeon with the implacable strength of a mountain in motion.

Her eyes were still new enough to life to widen in wonder at the world, but they looked out through a brass-trimmed slit in a helmet of burnished iron. Out and down. She towered over the tallest man in the village, Barnard Tinker, the man who'd built the machine she'd used to kill a devil and lead her village in rebellion.

Below the helmet was the heavy iron gorget, and below that, the machine's solid breastplate, covering the driver's cage and Heloise's body. Barnard had painted a red sigil across it, and again on the shield—a little girl, with a halo and wings, standing on a fallen devil's neck. The girl's hand was extended, palm outward, in the traditional pose of Palantines. Heloise felt the weight of her people's expectations every time she looked at it. She knew who she was, and it wasn't who Barnard, and the whole village, expected her to be.

The breastplate hung on a metal armature, long rods that formed a man-shaped cage around Heloise. Hung across it was more armor—pauldrons and vambraces, tassets and greaves, couters and sabbatons and the heavy, wicked gauntlets. But where the gaps on a suit of armor would be covered with mail, the machine admitted the empty air, and Heloise shivered as the cold breeze blew through the openings and caressed her bare skin.

"They are coming, your eminence, they will be here by sunset." It was the voice of Barnard's son, Guntar, so much like his father's that Heloise had to look down to confirm. He was red-faced, breathless. He'd leapt off one of Poch Drover's cart horses, taken for his reconnaissance. Poch raced to take the animal's reins, patting its lathered flanks and glaring at Guntar. The beast was made for slow hauling, not fast riding. It looked blown, and Poch couldn't keep the anguish off his face. The old man loved his horses.

Guntar took a knee before Heloise, and the rest of the villagers joined him, as if she were a lord, or a Pilgrim.

Or a holy Palantine, a devil-slayer, a savior and protector.

She had slain a devil, but her throat still tightened at the reverence in their eyes. They had known her since she was a babe-in-arms. They were her home and her family. She wanted them to hold her, to tell her that everything would be all right.

But everything will not be all right, she thought, *and if it is to be even a little bit right, then it is for me to make it so.*

For all their fervor, the villagers around her were still an untrained rabble with barely three helmets between them, armed with pruning hooks and pitchforks, here and there a rusty pike or sword left over from their days as a levy in the Old War against Ludhuige and his Red Banners. They were old men, the wives and children of old men. Their names were Sald Grower, Ingomer Clothier and Edwin Baker. None had the name "Soldier." A few, like her father and Sigir, the village Maior, were veterans of the Old War, but Heloise knew that levies attended to their trades until they were called to fight. Soldiering was not their life's work.

And the Order would be there by sunset. Heloise thought of Sigir's words after the Knitting. *The Order speaks of ministry, but it is the paint over the board. The wood beneath is killing. It is what they train to do, it is what they are equipped to do, it is all they do.*

The rebels had just one thing: the war-machine Heloise drove, the giant suit of metal and leather that made her stronger and taller than the two most powerful men in the village combined. This new war-machine was made for her, her arms and legs fitting perfectly inside its metal limbs, her movements become its own. But as powerful as the machine was, it hadn't been enough to save Heloise's best friend, the love of her life. Her gaze swept the throng, ready to follow her into war. *I couldn't save Basina,* she wanted to shout, *what makes you think I can save you?* When they'd beaten the Order before, they'd had a wizard with them. Now, there was only Heloise, her machine, and the supposed favor of the divine Emperor.

"Sigir, a word," Samson said. His eyes flicked between the Maior and Barnard, his lips working beneath his gray beard.

"Samson, there is no time," Barnard snapped. "You heard Guntar. The Order will be here soon. This"—he gestured to the massive war-machine—"is too loud. Too big and too shiny. The Order will know we're here from a league off."

"I wasn't talking to you," Samson shot back, then turned to the Maior. "Sigir, please. Now."

Heloise looked down at her father. He was so like the Maior, both men thick-necked and thick-fingered, with heavy paunches that overhung their belts and shoulders broadened from the work that attended village life. Sigir wore long mustaches, but for that and the gold chain of Sigir's office, they could have been brothers. It had only been a few nights ago that her father's approval had meant everything to her, but the fight with the devil had changed everything. A part of her recoiled from the thought of defying him, but Barnard was right, there was no time.

"Father, it's fine."

"It is *not* fine," Samson practically spat, his face reddening. "This is the other side of the sun from fine."

"Samson, please." Sigir gestured at the villagers all around them. *Everyone is watching,* the Maior's face said.

Leuba, Heloise's mother, was among the crowd. She lent truth to the old adage that a couple married long enough began to look like one another—heavy like her husband, thick-fingered and wide-cheeked. But where Samson was thunder, Leuba was the silence after its passing, and she kept her peace and let her husband speak, wringing the hem of her skirts in her hands. But Heloise remembered her mother's fierce fire when the village had thought to cast her father out after his fight with the Order. *I'll stand at your side and the town fathers will have to look me in the eye as they speak their piece,* her mother had said, eyes flashing. *Might be that will make them think kinder of what they say.*

Samson sighed, swallowed. "Barnard is right, the machine is too big, too loud, and too shiny. So we move it *back, away* from the road. We can have an ambush without risking the life of my daughter."

Heloise wanted to agree with him. Here was the chance to step down from behind that sigil, shrug off the weight of it all. She wasn't a Palantine. What business did she have leading an ambush against the Order?

"Samson," Sigir said.

"No," Samson said, "I understand that . . . much has happened in the past few days, but this is *wrong,* Sigir. You are the *Maior.* We follow *you.*"

Sigir threw an arm around Samson's shoulder, steering him away from the crowd of villagers. "By the Throne, will you be quiet? The village's will hangs by a thread as it is!" The Maior was trying to keep his voice low, but in the shocked silence Heloise could hear him as clearly as if he had shouted.

"She's my daughter!" Samson made no effort at quiet. "It is for me to say whether she fights! And I say—"

"Father!" Heloise took a step toward him, forgetting for a moment that she was in the giant war-machine. The metal leg moved with her, a lurching step that sent the villagers nearest her scattering.

Sigir's grip was tight around Samson's shoulders as he steered him further away from the villagers. Heloise followed and Barnard and his sons came with her, Leuba trailing behind them.

"I am your father," Samson was speaking to her now, "and I am through with this . . . foolishness. A machine may make you strong, but it does *not* make you a Palantine. You are my daughter and you will come down from that thing and away."

"Samson," Sigir tightened his grip on her father's shoulders. "Enough, she is—"

Samson shook off his grip. "No! You are the Maior. It is to you to uphold the law, but she is my daughter, and she will do as I say. The village follows—"

"Samson, you Throne-cursed fool!" Sigir threw up his hands, pointed a trembling finger at Heloise. "Do you think you can go on as if the veil was not torn? As if she didn't just do what *no one* has ever done in all the days of our people? The village follows *her*, you blockhead. We are to ambush the *Order*. Do you think for a moment that we can do that without a war-machine? Do you think we can do it without the people's hearts united behind their savior? She *must* lead us, or we must flee, and I do not like our chances on the run. Not now, with the Order so close."

And there it was. Heloise's stomach tightened. *He's right. I have to do this. I must at least act the Palantine or we are all finished.*

"I don't care," Samson said, "that is my decision and it is final. She comes down now. She is my daughter."

"Basina," Barnard's voice was low and dangerous, "was my daughter. And she is dead."

The dread certainty that she must defy her father solidified. *Basina is dead. The Order is coming. Both are my fault. I have to make this right.*

"Killed by the devil!" Samson shouted back. "And the devil is dead. Avenged by my daughter. Heloise deserves life for that, if nothing else."

"Everyone deserves life," Sigir said, "and that's why everyone must fight."

"I will be fine, Father," Heloise said. "Now just stop . . ."

But Samson was striding forward, grasping the machine's metal legs and scrambling up. Heloise jerked back in surprise, the machine jerking with her. Barnard and Sigir pulled away from the sudden movement, but Samson managed to hold on. "What are you doing?"

"I am taking you out of there," Samson said, "and once I have, you are going over my knee until you learn obedience, by the Throne."

"Father, no! Stop . . ."

But Samson was not deterred, he reached the machine's metal cuisse and thrust a hand behind the breastplate, fumbling for the strap that held Heloise against the leather cushion. Heloise reached a hand over to stop him, stopped as she realized the machine's arm was matching her movement, the heavy metal shield dangerously close to her father's head. She was struggling to free her arms from the control straps to safely push him away when Barnard stepped forward, seized Samson by the collar of his shirt, and sent him tumbling in the dirt. Leuba cried out and ran to her husband's side. Samson swatted her helping hands away and rose to his elbows, cheeks bright red.

"She's a devil-slayer and a Palantine." Barnard's voice was flat. Barnard and Samson had been friends their own whole lives, but now Barnard hefted his hammer as Samson got to one knee. "She's not your little girl anymore. She is the Emperor's instrument now."

"You think," Samson bit off each word, pushing Leuba behind him, "that I won't kill you, should you stand between me and my daughter?"

"No," Barnard said, "I think you won't kill me because you

cannot." The huge tinker was a head taller than her father, his gray-shot black beard trimmed short to accommodate the forge-fires that had lit his entire working life. Working beside those fires had made him as strong as he was tall, more bear than man, and still little more than a child in the shadow of the war-machine. His sons stood at his side, each nearly as big as their father, each wielding a two-handed forge hammer heavy enough to fell an ox with a single blow.

Samson stood, and Heloise knew he would try the matter even if it cost him his life. Clodio had spoken of love, of how life without it was but a shadow of life, but Heloise could see now that a father's love could drive him mad. Could even cost him his life. "I won't let you send my daughter to her death."

"My daughter is *dead*," Barnard seethed. "Yours can fight."

Samson took a step and Heloise stepped with him, moving the machine around the Tinker men to stand it between them and her father. "Father, please!"

"You can either help us to fight," Sigir said, "or you can delay until the Order comes and we are caught unawares."

"You're mad," Samson said, looking daggers at Sigir and the Tinkers. "You're all mad!"

"She killed a devil," Guntar said, "she's a Palantine."

"Look at this!" Samson stabbed a finger at the red sigil Barnard had painted on the machine's breast. "Do you see wings on my daughter?"

"Blasphemy," said Gunnar, Barnard's other son, and stabbed a finger of his own. "You shame the Emperor, denying His chosen."

"You're lucky you're her father, Samson," Barnard said, "else I might . . ."

"What?" Samson's laugh was forced. "You'll box my ears and turn out my pockets? You'll kill me in front of my own wife and child? By the Throne, do your worst."

"You'll have to kill me, too, you animal," Leuba stepped around her husband, face white with fury. "I've known you since you was a boy, Tinker, and you'll have to kill me in front of your sons before I let you hurt my husband."

"Sacred Throne, *enough*!" Sigir shouted. "You want my word? You want the word of the Maior of Lutet? I will give it, and it is this: Heloise fights. Palantine or no, we need her and we do not have time to convene a council on the matter. This little display has sapped the village's spirits enough, I am sure. Come, Heloise, let's figure out a way to get the machine concealed."

"Damn you, Sigir!" Samson said. "I will never forgive you for this, so long as you live!"

"I suppose I can live with that"—Sigir shrugged—"and this gives us all, including Heloise, the best chance to go *on* living."

Heloise turned to follow the Maior back to the knot of villagers, and Samson moved to intercept her. He stopped as the Tinkers stepped to bar his way, raising their hammers. "Don't," Barnard growled.

"Please, Heloise." Leuba sounded on the verge of tears. "I don't know what I'd do if I lost you. We only want to protect you."

"You can't protect me, not from this." She turned to her father. "Don't you understand? Basina is dead. I *have* to do this."

But she could see in his eyes that he didn't understand. It was a moment before Heloise mustered the strength to look away, ignoring the strangled choke her father made. He only wanted to protect her, but the Order was coming. And Sigir was right, they had to fight, not to win, but to *live. I may be a girl, Papa,* she thought fiercely at him, as if the intensity of it could make him hear and understand, *but I am the one they've chosen to follow.*

Samson and Leuba stood apart, watching as Sigir directed the villagers to gather branches and clods of earth to drape over the machine. Barnard and his sons kept a close eye on Samson, ready to move if he tried to intervene. The villagers had clearly over-heard much of the conversation, and their allegiance was clear. They circled around Heloise, studiously ignoring Samson, when they weren't glaring daggers in his direction. The sole exceptions were Poch Drover and Sald Grower, who stood apart, casting wor-ried glances over at Heloise's father, but not daring to move against the Tinkers.

Heloise could feel her father's eyes on her back. She could feel his gaze sapping her will. *What if he's right? What if I can't lead them? What if I can't fight?* She pushed the thought away. In a bro-ken machine, she had killed a devil. Who knew what she could do in this machine, whole as it was? *Not whole*, Heloise thought as she looked down at her right arm, *the machine, maybe, but not me.* The stump of her wrist hooked the control strap, though she winced as she pulled experimentally and the leather put pressure on the bandage. Barnard hadn't bothered to affix a weapon to the war-machine's metal fist, fearing the extra weight would add to the hurt. She needed time to heal, but the Order was coming now.

Some of the villagers saw her looking at the machine's empty right hand, at the stump within. They shuffled, uneasy. *Fear's a deadly thing, Heloise,* Barnard had said. *It can drain a person of all their strength, make them weak before their enemies. That's how we were until you showed us different. But we see now, and we are not afraid anymore, so long as you are with us.*

She wrenched her gaze away from the bloody bandages and forced herself to meet the eyes of the assembled throng. "I am with you," she said, "after the devil, the Order will be nothing."

In answer, the villagers bowed their heads or tugged their fore-locks and raced to cover the machine with more branches and earth.

"Now, you all listen to me," Sigir said as they worked. "Should . . . things go badly for us . . ."

"Blasphemy," Barnard said, his eyes never leaving Samson. "We have—"

"Will you shut your yob for a gnat's whisper, Tinker!" Sigir said. "The Emperor is with us, to be sure, but He will no doubt smile on a well-formed plan. Faith isn't always rushing in with your balls hanging out."

Barnard opened his mouth to reply, but Samson cut him off. "You got what you wanted, Barnard. Heloise is fighting. Let the Maior speak!"

Barnard looked up at Heloise, cheeks red, waiting for her direction. She would never get used to this man, who had known her since she was a baby, who could break her with a twist of his fingers, looking to her for orders. She swallowed the discomfort and nodded. "Let us hear the Maior out."

Sigir spoke quickly, "Should the enemy take the day, we go to the fens."

Barnard shook his head. "The frogging clans won't have us if they know we've taken arms against the Order. They're the most pious folk in the valley."

"We don't need them to shelter us, and we won't go all the way into the mire," Sigir went on. "The fens are broken ground. Close enough for us to make it on foot, but the mud will suck the shoes off the horses and the holes will snap their legs. If the Order wants to come for us, they'll have to come on foot. In all that armor, they'll be slow. We know the ground, and they don't. It's the best place to fight in skirmish order."

"What do we know of skirmishing?" Samson asked. "We're trained to the pike, formed and well commanded."

"We'll have to learn, won't we?" Sigir said. "If it comes to it, I mean."

They made little headway hiding the machine. Some tried to weave the branches into a lattice that could hold the earth, others simply piled them on, or thrust them into the frame. Some stayed put. Most didn't. After a quarter candle they'd succeeded mostly in piling a heap of brush around the machine's metal feet, and smearing dirt on Heloise's shift, face, and all over the interior of the driver's cage.

"This isn't working," Sigir finally said. "We'll need to dig a hole."

"That will take too long," Barnard gestured to the enormous machine. He stomped the frozen ground. "It's hard as stone here."

"If all of us pitch in," Sigir said, "we can get it done in time."

"Begging your pardon, Maior," Sald Grower said, "we can't. Even if we had shovels for every man, it'd take days to bury something that big."

Barnard snorted. "We don't need to bury her," he said. "She can run faster than a horse in that. By the time they know she's awaiting them, it'll be too late."

"That is madness," Samson shouted. "Barnard, Sigir, *please*. It's one thing to have her fight. It's quite another to have her rushing into battle like a . . ."

All around her, villagers were throwing in their considered opinions, shouting to be heard among the others.

"It was to be an ambush!" her father was shouting.

"She is a Palantine! She needs no ambush!" Barnard yelled.

Heloise was no soldier, but she knew this confusion wouldn't beat the Order. Everyone was giving orders, and no one was listening.

"Shut it!" Heloise's words rang through the din before she realized she had yelled them.

The silence dragged on, and Heloise realized with a start that they were waiting for her command. "I . . . I think I know what to do. Follow me."

She took a step, then another, then another, and the war-machine took them with her, the crowd parting to let her pass, then closing to follow her through the overgrown thicket and back out onto the road that led to her village. It was little more than a wide track, stretching out in a low valley bordered by two gently sloping rises. Both were well concealed, the thicket on one side, and a nearly solid wall of trees on the other.

She felt the machine's heavy tread sinking into the softer ground, still frozen, but warmed by the sparse traffic, the clods of horse dung, and the break in the canopy that laid it bare to the sun.

Samson was at her elbow in an instant, Barnard coming with him. "Leave me be, you great pill!" Samson shouted at the tinker, "I'm not going to try to take her out of the . . ."

Heloise ignored them both, dropping the machine to one knee, raising the shield high over her head.

She could hear the sharp intake of breath, feel the crowd backing away from her. She brought the machine's shield arm down with all its engine-driven strength. The point of the shield careered off a stone just under the surface of the soil, sending up a shower of sparks and making a sound like two empty pots banged together. But that only served to drive the shield point to one side, and it sank deep into the earth, digging a furrow almost two hand-spans deep.

The ground was hard, but it was not equal to the engine's brutal strength. Together with the heavy weight of the iron shield, the ground broke apart, clods of earth spraying as Heloise dug.

For a moment, the village watched in confusion, and then Sigir was on his knees beside her, clawing at the earth with his hands. Barnard soon joined him in the rapidly deepening pit. Gunnar and Guntar followed, swinging their great forge hammers, breaking up rocks and roots. At last, all the village pitched in, scraping and digging with shield edges, knives and swords, and here and there an actual shovel.

As the hole became shoulder deep, Barnard began waving some of them off. "We'll need to cover it. Weave a screen of branches."

"Won't hold up under a horse," Sald muttered.

"Sald, you're a Throne-cursed grower," Barnard said, "what do you know of horses?"

Heloise glanced up at the road. It was more than wide enough for a column of riders to pass without moving over the hole she would be hiding in. She forced herself to return to her digging. The sun was sinking beneath the horizon, it was too late to turn back now.

Some of the villagers went scurrying off to comply with Barnard's order. Heloise noticed that Samson was among them. *It's better this way. The less he's about, the less you'll be tempted to give in to him.*

They made good progress, but every moment Heloise thought they were moving fast enough, they hit a man-sized rock, or a root as thick around as her wrist, lost more precious time. The machine's great size had been a comfort to her before she'd started digging, and now she cursed it for needing a pit so deep to hide it.

The shadows were growing long when Guntar finally leaned on his hammer and cursed. "It can't be long now," he said, "if we don't get out of this road, we'll be ridden down."

"Then we make our stand," Barnard said, "and die on our feet."

"How many standing dead men have you seen?" Sigir asked. "An ambush is our only chance. If we cannot catch them unawares, we should run, come at them another time."

"And let them burn the village?" Gunnar's voice was heated.

"What else . . ." Sigir began, and Heloise knew that once again she would have to stop the men from arguing.

It took her a moment to find the strength. The digging had made her tired in her bones. Her stump throbbed, the bandages soaked through with fresh blood where the wound had reopened. She felt a flash of heat across her forehead, sharp enough to make her sweat, followed by a shiver. *It's fever.* She pushed the thought away. If it was, there was nothing to do for it now.

The men argued, and she glanced at the hole, still woefully shallow, but maybe . . .

She put confidence into her voice. "It's deep enough."

The men stopped fighting, raised their heads to her. They looked at one another, then at the shallow hole, then finally back to her. "Your eminence," Sigir began, "you cannot possibly . . ."

"Not to stand, no," Heloise said, walking the machine on its knees into the hole, praying she had guessed right. The metal frame groaned as she folded her legs and sat on her heels, the machine shaping itself to mimic her posture. She leaned forward at her waist, tucking the machine's head between its metal knees. The engine's bulk blocked out most of the sun, so that she could see only the dimmest reflection of light off the metal tops of the machine's knees. "You can't see me from the road, can you?"

"No." Barnard's voice, slow and deep. "Praise the Throne, we cannot."

Heloise stifled a sigh of relief. "Then cover me up. There's not much time."

"Not yet!" Her mother's voice. She winced as she heard Leuba scramble down, leaning on the machine's shoulder. The machine shuddered as she shrugged off Barnard's hand, trying to pull him back. "Leave me be!" She tried for a kiss, but there was no way to reach her, so she settled for touching her shoulder. "Oh, my dove. Be careful. I love you," she whispered. Her father's weight settled on the machine's opposite shoulder. The same touch, the same words. Heloise choked back tears and nodded. *Not now. I can't be your daughter now.*

Heloise heard the scraping of branches as the latticework was dragged toward her. A weight on the machine again, much heavier this time, accompanied by a loud clang.

Heloise sawed her head to her right, saw Barnard strapping a brass-bound, metal box to the machine's shoulder. "What are you doing?" She asked.

"The devil's head," Barnard said reverently, cinching the straps down and patting the box's huge brass lock, "will keep the Emperor's eye turned toward us. It is yours, your eminence, and you will carry it high as you lead us to victory."

The box would block her view to one side, and the thought of the devil's severed head so close to her made her stomach lurch, but as she opened her mouth to argue, they dragged the lattice over her, and all was shrouded in darkness. Tiny pinpricks of sunlight dotted the pitted surface of the machine's metal legs, but beyond that, the world vanished.

"Wait until they have all gone past, your eminence," Sigir said as they scraped earth over. "You will rise behind them and then we will strike from the sides. They will be trapped, and if Emperor is willing, we will triumph."

The scraping and thumping of earth being piled on her grew more muffled as the cover of woven branches filled in. The pinpricks of light vanished one by one, until at last Heloise could hear nothing at all, and she was alone with the darkness and the stifling chill of the pit.

Now, Sald's words seemed wrong. They had piled so much earth atop her that it would easily hold ten horses. So much that she would never see the sun again.

The tiny space stank of seethestone. She stifled a cough and shut her stinging eyes, squeezing out tears. Her skin tingled and itched as the caustic smoke, with nowhere else to go, turned on her. The only sound was her own short, gasping breaths, so loud in the tight space that the entire Imperial army could be marching over her back and she wouldn't hear them.

This was stupid, useless. She couldn't breathe, couldn't see, couldn't hear. She wanted only to stand up, throw off the oppressive weight of the earth.

She felt a tremor. No more than a ripple of the earth across her back, a pebble shaken loose to drop against the machine's metal knee. It was followed by another, and another, until the ground around her came alive with rumbling, the earth overhead vibrating under tramping feet and hooves.

The Order. They were here.

She could hear muffled voices, the creaking of leather harness, the jangling of chains. She tensed, waiting for the hoofbeats to pass, so that she could rise up behind the column, cutting off their retreat.

She felt a sharp pounding against the machine's metal back. Rhythmic, steady.

The latticework was holding. The Order was riding over her. She tried to count the hoofbeats, to guess the number of animals passing, to get a count of how many enemy she would face. She tried to stifle the itching in her throat, swallow the urge to cough, and waited for . . .

A horse stumbled. Earth cascaded around her.

Shouts, hooves skittering sideways, the drumming of feet. The column had been alerted, halted. The latticework of branches, even with the thick layer of earth, had not been enough to hold a warhorse's weight with an armored rider on its back. If Heloise rose now, she would emerge at their head, giving them a clear road to retreat, and the element of surprise gone.

She heard scraping above her, men straining to pry the lattice-work away. In moments, they would find her. *You can either die down here on your knees, or up on your feet, breathing the air.*

It was an easy choice. Heloise dug in her heels and jerked her legs straight. The machine shuddered as it rose, metal back and shoulders exploding upward, sending the latticework spinning away. She heard men and horses screaming. Light and spraying earth blinded her, but not so much that she couldn't see two men and a horse flying through the air, sailing head over foot into a column of Pilgrims. The horses spooked, and the Pilgrims, desperate to control them, had no time to gawk at the war-machine in their midst. There was no time to count them, but their numbers seemed endless, at least a hundred riders, thick leather armor making them huge beneath their gray cloaks.

The men and horse that Heloise had thrown came down in their ranks, knocking men from their mounts and sending them sprawling in the mud, cursing. Heloise blinked, her eyes adjusting, her vision still blurry. The column was a splintered mass of plunging horses and shouting men. Most still had their flails on their shoulders, if they hadn't dropped them in the chaos.

She wouldn't get a better chance than this.

"The Throne!" Heloise shouted, and charged.